Day Trips to Heaven

To Jean

Love + Light

Tjhobbs

Day Trips to Heaven

Adventures in the Afterlife

T J Hobbs

A record of this publication is available from the British Library.

ISBN 978-1-907203-99-2

Typesetting by Wordzworth Ltd
www.wordzworth.com

Cover design by Titanium Design Ltd
www.titaniumdesign.co.uk

Printed by Lightning Source UK
www.lightningsource.com

Cover image © Sylvie Gotti

Published by Local Legend
www.local-legend.co.uk

I thank Stefan Zurich for uttering the words that
inspired this novel and his grandmother,
my good friend Joy Seal, who told them to me.

About This Book

There are times – especially when life is hard – when every one of us wonders what Heaven might be like... Here's your chance to find out! Ethan is learning the ropes as a spiritual guide and not finding it at all easy, despite the help of his lovely mentor Danielle and Archangel Haniel. Join him on his rollercoaster trial runs as he is allowed to bring a few deserving souls from Earth for a preview of the afterlife.

This charming book is full of gentle humour and spiritual wisdom. It is a compassionate account of the lessons each one of us needs to learn during our journey on the Earth... letting go of pain, discovering our life's purpose and caring for the planet.

The Author

T J Hobbs is a natural health care practitioner who has been working on her own spiritual development for twenty-four years. She is especially drawn to Native American and Celtic shamanism. *Day Trips to Heaven* is her exciting debut novel.

Several other spiritual novels, short stories and children's picture books are in progress and she also really loves science fiction; a series of Solar Star novels are on the way.

Her other interests are horse riding, Tai-chi, travel and photography. She lives in Hampshire, England.

Her website is *www.tjhobbs.co.uk*

Contents

★

CHAPTER 1

Ethan Finds his Feet

The truck lurched perilously towards the sheer drop into the river and Ethan's heart skipped a beat as he grabbed the door frame while Tomas fought with the steering wheel and somehow managed to keep them on the mountain road. Ethan sank back into his seat and blew out his cheeks in relief.

"That was too close, Tomas," he said, and the small sharp-featured driver nodded as he grinned at back at him.

"Sorry, my friend, but the road..." he shrugged his bony shoulders and Ethan sighed.

It was true that the roads were not a very high priority in this war-torn country right now but he also suspected that this road had never been much better. It was a dangerous route even before the war but now it was one of the only ways left to get supplies into the village and hospital so they had no choice but to use it. In their truck they carried vital medicines, food and water which were all in short supply, and Ethan worried that it wouldn't be long before this vital link was also mined and useless to them.

The war was not going well and even though he was a foreigner and worked as a medic, not a soldier, he doubted it would matter much if their position were overrun. He sighed again as he pushed his ragged dark brown hair off his sweaty face and tried not to think what the future might hold.

In the last few weeks he had seen more horrors than he'd ever wished to and even though he was almost a qualified doctor the injuries bombs and bullets inflicted on human flesh sickened him. He had never seen anything like this in England where he was born and bred, and he'd come here, so he thought, to help out in a hospital in the Balkans. Instead he'd been sent to a battle front to treat the endless flow of casualties there, but the lack of medical supplies and operating theatres just thwarted his efforts and sapped his strength. He was so tired of the fighting - not just the war but the infighting amongst the doctors too, so much so that he was more than ready to get out of here and go home. It was only the thought of leaving people like Tomas and his family to the mercy of their enemies that kept him here.

He had arrived only three months ago, idealistic and thinking he could make a difference, but now he wondered what he was doing and if he had actually helped anyone. Although he was twenty-five, he didn't look it with his boyish handsome face and gangling build. He could pass as a teenager and this had made it hard for him to be taken seriously as a competent doctor; the self-appointed boss of the hospital certainly didn't treat him with any resect at all. Take this trip for instance: he shouldn't be wasting his time riding shotgun in the truck when he could be operating on patients or treating the wounded. But no, he was told that he'd be more useful doing this and he felt angry and frustrated. However well he had performed so far, Doctor Radic still would not let him work without looking over his shoulder and criticising everything he did. It was driving him mad.

As the truck rumbled on, throwing him from side to side, his brown eyes began to close for a few seconds as the lack of sleep finally caught up with him. The truck jolted and rocked violently, causing his head to snap back and hit the seat rest, waking him from his slumber.

"What was that?" he asked Tomas.

Tomas shrugged. "Just rocks, don't worry," he told him and Ethan turned his head to look out of the window. There was a brilliant flash of white light that blinded him and then a roaring sound followed by a wave of flames and heat. Before he had time to scream, he felt himself lifted off the seat and thrown into the air at great speed.

His last thoughts were of the waste of it all, of disappointment and regret, and then nothing.

The pain he had been expecting never came and he found himself momentarily in darkness. Then a spot of gold light appeared and gradually grew into a tunnel big enough for him to walk into. A small hand touched his arm and a feminine voice with a French accent spoke to him, making him jump.

"Cherie, it is over now," she said, and it suddenly dawned on him that he was no longer in his physical body. A wave of panic hit him and he pulled away from her, turning to defend himself from whatever lurked in the darkness. But instead of an enemy he found a friend.

Standing there was the petite blonde girl, with bright blue eyes and a smile to die for, whom he had met so many times in his dreams that he felt he knew her. She had always come to him when he needed her and listened to him without judgment - a rare thing these days - and then she would help him work out what he should do. Now, somehow, she was here again at the time of his most desperate need.

"Danielle, what's happened?" he asked her. She smiled sadly at him and took his hand.

"Ethan, the truck hit a mine and your physical life is now over. But all is not lost, Cherie, as I am going to take you to a much better place where there is no war going on." He gazed at her in shock, but as he looked around he knew she was telling him the truth.

"Are we going to Heaven?" he asked, as he had been brought up to believe that if he were good enough that's where he would end up. She smiled and turned to look up the glowing tunnel before answering him.

"Come with me and you will find out," she told him. The alternative was staying in the dark, which he certainly didn't want to do, so he allowed her to lead him along the tunnel. As soon as he entered it, he felt the love hit him and he recognised it.

"I've been here before," he said, and Danielle laughed.

"Yes, you have, many times, but now you can stay if you want to and help people from here." He frowned and wondered what she meant, but it didn't take long to find out.

Ethan sighed inwardly as learning to be a guide like Danielle was turning out to be a lot harder than he had thought. He looked around the open air classroom in the beauty of the sunken garden surrounded by perfumed flowers, with its classical Greek-style sculptures of inspiring humans in white marble, but he didn't feel inspired at all. As the others got up from their benches, excitement and enthusiasm shining on their faces, all he felt was heaviness deep inside his very being.

He had just sat through a lecture by Archangel Haniel about the importance of non-interference. Wasn't he supposed to interfere? Isn't that what the job was all about? And archangels were not as he expected them to be either. They had no wings for a start; that idea, he was informed, had been a medieval invention and for some reason this upset him greatly. Instead, she looked deceptively human: taller than usual and with a glow of perfection around her, from her golden skin tones and silky blonde hair to her violet coloured eyes, she was the most beautiful woman he had ever seen.

Haniel looked at him, the only student remaining, and hid a smile as she had seen it all before. In every class there was one student who found the job of guide confusing, even contradictory, yet most of the time it was that very student who, once graduated, became the best. It was tough, she didn't deny that, and most of the time you were unappreciated and even ignored, but it was vital too.

The Creator, from the beginning of time, had understood that life in its many and varied guises needed support in order to grow and develop into higher forms of existence; so guides would always be needed. But it wasn't the right job for everyone and it certainly wasn't easy. The hardest job in the universe is being a guide for someone who is totally unaware of one's existence. Haniel moved to Ethan's side, knowing that now was the time for her to give a little extra.

"Is there something I can help you with?" she asked politely.

Ethan looked up at Haniel and was momentarily speechless; he still had trouble dealing with her appearance as he hadn't been prepared for angels to look so, well, human. She stood over six feet tall but was so slight in build that she appeared to be made up of mist, not flesh. 'Etheric' was the word he wanted to use for her, as she seemed to shimmer from the inside out. He looked at her heart-shaped face and bright eyes.

"Yes, I rather hope you can."

"Where there is hope, there are possibilities," she said, and smiled at the frown that had appeared on Ethan's handsome boyish face. She felt an urge to ruffle his dark brown hair. He had chosen to appear as he had been before the explosion with his tousled hair, pale skin and brown eyes.

"Isn't it 'where there's life, there's hope'?" Ethan queried.

"But there is always life, it cannot die. No need for hope there. That's Rule Number One," she said. Ethan mentally kicked himself; he was still thinking too much like a human, with all those preconceived beliefs.

"Of course, yes, I'm sorry," he muttered.

"There's nothing to be sorry about." She paused then asked, "So, what is it I can help you with?" Ethan suppressed the desire to sigh again.

"Everything," he said instead. Haniel cocked her head to one side.

"Oh dear. Well, if it's everything, perhaps you could tell me one thing, so we have somewhere to start."

She sat down on the bench beside her pupil and prepared herself for a long session, but being in this peaceful garden with the scents of so many different flowers and the air filled with birdsong, it was no hardship at all. There was quite a wait for Ethan to sort out where he should begin but finally he realised what he really wanted to say the most. He took a deep breath.

"I don't think I can do this."

Haniel's expression didn't change as she looked at him in her usual compassionate manner and, for a few seconds, she didn't reply.

"I see," she said finally. "Well, you always have the choice to drop out of the course, you know that?" Ethan nodded, so she continued. "Yet you were chosen as someone who had reached the stage of development where being another's guide would be the next step in your own journey."

"I have?" he queried, surprised.

"Yes, of course you have. Over the past few hundred years, you have lived many lives. Each one had its purpose, even if sometimes you never knew it or attained it, but you grew spiritually nevertheless and now you no longer need to return to Earth - although you can if you choose to. If you like, you have graduated, left the university and moved on here to the spirit world and now it is time to learn even more and eventually move on again. There are many rooms in the Creator's mansions and this stage is just one of them."

"So, it's a bit like starting back in kindergarten?"

"A bit," Haniel agreed, "except that you have already completed all that is necessary for you on the third-dimensional level. So now you need to learn new skills to help others. And because you haven't been here too long, you are perfectly placed to understand the problems and fears that abound on worlds such as Earth. We find that the best guides are those who haven't forgotten what it is like to be human."

Ethan sat quietly considering what he had been told; he was pleased that he had attained enough spiritual brownie points not to have to go back to Earth but he still wasn't sure he was quite ready to guide someone else. He looked up into the patient face of Haniel.

6

"I see what you mean, but can I help anyone? I mean, it's so complicated and there are so many rules. I don't want to make matters worse instead of better." He looked down at his hands in a dejected manner. Haniel's face twitched ever so slightly at the young soul's dejection. He felt the burden of responsibility even before he'd been given a charge to guide and yet, ironically, this was a good sign. Unlike some of his more confident classmates who saw their task as an adventure and exciting, Ethan unconsciously understood that it was far from that.

"I know it seems a little overwhelming at the moment, but you have a lot still to learn." Ethan sat looking down and didn't reply, so Haniel continued by asking him some questions. "Ethan, what do you consider causes the greatest problems for people on Earth?" He frowned, unsure what answer to give as he didn't really understand the question; Haniel guessed as much and smiled. "What I mean is, speaking from your own experiences on Earth, what influence or emotions caused you the most pain and difficulty?" The frown on his face disappeared.

"Oh, I see," he said, then considered carefully before he answered. "I suppose the biggest block people have is fear."

"Yes, you are correct," Haniel nodded. "There is so much that people fear and then they seem to like to add guilt too, which increases their fears a hundred-fold."

She sighed now. She was of the angelic realms and therefore had never been incarnated like Ethan; as an archangel, she had visited Earth on occasions but she still didn't really understand the feelings people experienced there. It was impossible for her kind, that's why they didn't guide souls who were still on the third-dimensional plane. He knew all about fear, but now he was in the spirit world he couldn't believe he'd been so stupid. On Earth everything was so different, full of fear: fear of being alone but too scared to really live, fear of the dark but unable to go to the light… The list was endless and, ultimately, pointless. The fears he had believed in so diligently really didn't exist. In the bright light of spirit, there is nothing to fear.

"If only I'd known that then," he thought. Haniel smiled.

"You did know it then. Deep down inside, everyone does, it's just allowing yourself to remember and to believe, that is the problem."

Ethan wasn't surprised by having his thoughts answered when he hadn't spoken, but what Haniel said made him pause; he had to admit that she was right. At certain times, he was sure he'd been given a glimpse of Heaven and, for a while, his life had been abundantly joyful and happy. Then he'd lose it and slowly fall back into a state of greyness that would envelop him, keeping him from the light. But those tiny glimpses had never really prepared him for the beauty and peace he found now that he had returned home. Everywhere was perfect, like the many gardens, all laid out without a dead flower or weed anywhere. There were also towns and cities but no pollution or rubbish, just glorious buildings of every period in human history, interspersed with wild landscapes and wonderful creatures - there were even dragons in Heaven. It was familiar, but then it should be; inbetween his learning opportunities, he had been here many hundreds of times before. This time it had been a bit different, though, as he was staying and had been asked if he'd like to help others. He had readily agreed.

Since that first day, he had been working hard to learn all he could to be a guiding hand to those still on the pathway, as he had been, but the job description hadn't been at all like he'd imagined. He thought he'd already know a lot of it from working with his own guides in many lifetimes before; yet, like most things, the reality is far from the fantasy. He turned back to Haniel.

"You see, I don't feel I'll be much good at this."

"Why not?"

"I suppose," he ventured, "because I'd want to help too much."

"Ah, now we are getting somewhere," Haniel said quietly. "Many times I have heard others say what you have just said."

"And what did you reply?"

"That there are many ways to help," she said, smiling. "Sometimes a word will change a life around. A whisper in the wind can change the perspective of your charge and set them back on the right path for them."

"And I'd be allowed to do that?" Ethan asked, still confused on how far he could go when guiding another. Haniel nodded.

"Yes, you can, because your charge has free will. They can either hear the message and discard it or hear the message and act on it. That is the difference. You are not telling them what they should do, you are just mentioning a possibility, another option if you like, but the choice is theirs and theirs alone."

"Yes, I see," he said softly, nodding.

"But you are not convinced?" Haniel asked, as she could feel the confusion and turmoil in Ethan's soul.

"I am convinced it can be done. In fact, I've heard those distant voices myself. But I'm not sure I'd know when and how I should throw in my tuppence-worth." Haniel laughed heartily at that and, for several minutes, Ethan sat waiting for her to recover.

"You little ones are most amusing," she said finally.

Ethan scowled; he didn't mean to amuse, he wanted answers, but in the spiritual realm questions rarely received answers, or not directly at least. The way it seemed to work was that the seeker went in search of his own answers, which Ethan secretly thought was a cop-out and very frustrating indeed.

Haniel knew what he thought and she understood. She was beginning to wonder if Ethan was to be one of those rare students who would benefit from being given the opportunity to help others on Earth now. Although this chance was used sparingly, sometimes it was just the right incentive to teach the most promising potential guides what could be accomplished, through giving others a glimpse of Heaven. She certainly believed that Ethan had the right stuff to be a great guide but he needed to increase his confidence and understand just how sensitive, even subtle, the guiding hand must be. Doing this would teach him so much that, the more she considered it, the more she knew Ethan had to do it or they would lose him for a long time. That would be a tragedy, as the people on Earth needed good guidance now more than at any other time in the last two thousand years. Changes had already begun and more and more people were turning back to the spirit for help; in turn, they needed good guidance to support them as they changed the world forever. So they couldn't afford to lose Ethan and he needed to be encouraged to complete his training. Haniel was going to help him if it was allowed, but this was not a gift Haniel herself could grant; it was the Creator's, though she was hopeful it would be given. She turned to her student.

"Ethan, I believe you would be a sensitive and conscientious guide but I also understand your concerns. I would like to help you, but to do so I have to ask permission."

Ethan frowned. "You have to ask permission?" he queried, as he had thought the archangels were the top dogs here. Haniel smiled.

"Yes, we are all made by one being, our Creator. As He made you so He made me and we are all His children. So to help you in the way I would like to, I must ask His permission."

"And you'd do that for me?"

"Yes, you are my student and my job is to serve you, to guide you and help you. And if I am allowed, I will help you to begin to understand the power, joy and love that guiding another brings."

"That would be awesome," he said, smiling, and Haniel laughed again.

Frank's stomach began to tighten into a by now familiar ball as he approached the front door of Home Fields House where his beloved Kathleen now resided. It wasn't that it was a terrible place, because it was a new purpose-built unit for twenty-four dementia and terminally ill patients, with great staff and a wonderful atmosphere. It was not so much the place but what he would encounter inside that got him so anxious and depressed. He also felt guilty, as he had not visited Kathleen yesterday; it was the first time since she was moved here a year ago. Not that she would even have noticed his absence, as she hadn't recognised him for well over a year now anyway, but he still felt guilty. All that Catholic upbringing, he thought. He sighed, took a deep breath and ran a hand through his still thick salt and pepper hair before opening the door and going inside. Kathleen was sitting on a sofa so he sat next to her and took her small frail hand in his. She had shrunk so much in the last year and he hardly recognised the energetic yellow-haired girl he had fallen in love with all those years ago. Then her green eyes had danced with mischief and laughter and her smile would light up the room; but now her eyes were dead and she never smiled.

"Hello Kathleen, it's me, Frank," he said softly in his southern Irish brogue. But she didn't seem to hear him as she sat still looking into the distance, although he wasn't sure she was actually seeing anything. As the saying goes, 'The lights are on but nobody is home', a very accurate description of how she was now and had been for months.

"Oh, Kathleen, where are you?" he said softly as a tear rolled down from his grey-blue eyes onto his sunken cheek. He wished this torture were over once and for all as he couldn't bear to see her like this and know that only worse was to come. "You'd be better off in Heaven, my love," he told her as he gently stroked her soft white hair, wondering if she knew he was there at all.

★

CHAPTER 2

The Special Mission

Haniel left him and now he wasn't sure what he was supposed to do, but he needed a breath of fresh air so he picked up his books and took a walk in the gardens as they were breath-taking in their vivid colours, so much brighter and fresher than any on Earth. There were trees of perfect shape, with leaves of multi-coloured hues under which pathways meandered. The gardens ranged from a very formal, yet tranquil, Japanese-inspired one complete with koi carp, to a wild, natural habitat full of delicate flowers. Ethan loved all of them but often found himself drawn to the wild meadows and the comfortable log that was so perfect on which to sit, and it was here that he found peace from the continuing thoughts that plagued him.

He was glad he didn't have to return to Earth anymore as it was a harsh place to be and the pain and suffering perpetrated down there was too much for him to bear. With eyes closed he remembered his last life and how he had been so tired sometimes that he hadn't cared if he'd died, just to be released from the fear all around him. He had tried to help but, in the end, he wasn't sure he could or would be allowed to and this had angered him. When death came on that bright, spring morning it was a blessing as he knew that love and peace awaited him and that was what his soul cried out for more than anything. Man's inhumanity to man had taken its toll on him and he'd been sickened by the pain and terror men could inflict on each other. He wanted nothing more to do with it; yet why, then, had he been so quick to volunteer to help others? It was a question he had begun to ask himself and he had no answer.

"Never volunteer," he muttered. "I should have remembered that."

But he wasn't very good at following that piece of advice, as he'd volunteered to help in the Balkans too! He wasn't sure if it was the worst decision he'd ever made or one of the best. Strange to think that, when on Earth people might automatically say it was a bad call; but from the point of view of Heaven, it wasn't - just another lesson in a long line of them and now he was back where there was no pain, sickness, fear or terror.

"Then why do I feel so down?" he asked himself. The answer flew into his head a second later.

"Because you still believe in the limitations you imposed on yourself."

He shot up straight and looked around him in surprise but saw no-one there, yet that message felt like it came from outside of him. He glanced around again just to make sure he was alone before he relaxed enough to consider the message he'd received. He didn't want to, but he had to agree that he did have some very strange beliefs when he lived on Earth, ones that now looked quite ludicrous from this new perspective, ones like he'd 'never make old bones'. He smiled - so silly - then he thought about that last life and the smile slowly faded.

"Hang on a minute, I was right," he said indignantly, realising that he was only twenty-five years old when he'd left that life. He sighed at this and then thought he heard someone giggling behind him, slowly turning around to find Danielle standing there. She looked just the same as always: a petite, almost fragile young woman with mischievous brilliant blue eyes and long thick blonde hair, wearing a floating purple dress that if anything accentuated her femininity and beauty. She saw his scowl and laughed again, putting her delicate hand over her mouth.

"I am sorry, Ethan, but you are so funny, my Cherie."

He raised his eyes up to the Heavens and she started to giggle all over again; a small smile tugged at the corners of his mouth, as her laugh was infectious, a light, tinkling sound that couldn't fail to lift the heart of even the most depressed man. She finally stopped giggling when she saw his smile.

"Ah, Cherie, that is better. Why so serious? You are free now, isn't that what you wanted?"

"What I wanted?" he frowned. "I don't understand." She smiled and shook her head in mock imitation.

"You are the most infuriating of men, Cherie," she said and giggled again. His frown deepened.

"I am? How?"

She looked him up and down as he didn't look any different to how he had on Earth, although he could have if he'd wanted to as there were no restraints on what form you took once back in the spirit world - if you wished, you didn't need any form at all. But most souls who had spent a great many lives on a physical world just felt more comfortable having a recognisable shape and Ethan had decided to stay as he was, at least until before the explosion. She sighed and sat down on the log and he joined her.

"Cherie, you tried so hard to get yourself killed. It was fascinating."

"I did?"

"Oh yes, you will never know how close you got on more than one occasion, but it wasn't your time then."

"So, you prevented it? I didn't think you could."

"I couldn't." She smiled. "If it was meant to be, when you reached one of those crossroads where you have the choice to stay or come back, I could not help you. It was your decision. So here we are. I could have shaken you so hard sometimes as you tried my patience, little one, oh yes you did." He was astonished by her words as he'd never realised just how awful it must have been for her to be his guide.

"I'm sorry, Danielle, to have been such a ... "

"Pain?" she interjected, a ghost of a smile on her delicate features. He nodded ruefully.

"Yes, maybe that is the right word. I apologise."

"I accept your gracious apology and have to say that even though you were a pain I learned some valuable lessons from trying to guide you - even though most of the time you were too stubborn to listen." He didn't quite know how to take that. Was it a compliment or an insult? He decided to let that go. "Well, my friend, now you have your wish and you are here. So what are you looking so sad about?"

As he thought how ironic the situation in which he now found himself was, considering what Danielle had been saying, a smile slowly transformed his features as he looked up at her.

"I'm trying to become a guide," he said.

For a moment she was stunned and then her eyes and mouth opened in surprise as it hit her and she began to giggle then laugh; this time he joined in. Finally, he got some small control over himself and spluttered, "I know, it's hilarious. There you were telling me what a terrible time I gave you and here am I wondering if I could ever do the job at all."

"Oh, Cherie," she nodded, "hasn't God got the strangest sense of humour?"

"Perverse, I call it," he muttered darkly. But being in the sunshine of her presence made up for all his trials and tribulations. She shook her blonde hair and her blue eyes sparkled with impish mischief.

"Now, Cherie, perhaps I can give you some advice?"

"Yes, please do," he said, eager for any help.

"Okay then, this is it: to be a good guide you need the patience of a saint, the love of an archangel and the strength of ten men. But as you have none of these qualities, run as fast as you can." He didn't know quite what to say to that and his mouth opened and shut several times until he eventually regained the art of talking.

"Are you serious?" he queried. She smiled.

"In a way I am. You see, Cherie, none of us has all of those qualities. If we did, we would have moved on up to the next level of learning. So we are here to learn these skills and being a guide tests your patience and compassion often to the limit and beyond. Believe me, it is not easy."

"Was I your first charge?" he asked, wondering if it got easier with practice.

"Good Lord, no, but you were one of my most challenging." She saw the dejection returning to his soul, so she patted his arm affectionately and added, "Cherie, you are honoured to be asked to guide another, so don't be too hasty in throwing this chance away as times are changing on Earth. You know in your heart that is true, even if at times it appears to be a more violent and ugly place, truly it is not. You are needed, Ethan, so much so that you mustn't be put off by a few setbacks. I know you as a fighter, not a quitter, so you must hang in there."

He nodded, as he agreed with most of what she had said. But he still couldn't shake off the feeling that he wasn't good enough for the task he'd been asked to do. For a while they sat in silence, listening to the breeze gently rustling the leaves in the trees. She didn't know what else to say to him though she did believe he'd be a good guide; but unless he believed that, it just wouldn't work. She racked her brains, trying to think of words of encouragement to persuade him to persevere.

"You know, Ethan, even when you're guiding someone else, you can ask for help too - you won't be on your own. Remember, when you were training to be a doctor you found working with geriatric patients very hard and, one evening, you sat down and asked for help and understanding?" He smiled and nodded his head.

"Yes, and you gave it to me."

"No, I didn't."

"You didn't?" He blinked in surprise. She shook her head. "Then who did? I knew someone was there, as I sat in the relatives' room trying to think straight. I knew someone else was there."

"Yes, you're right, but it wasn't me. It was the spirit of a doctor who had passed over a few years ago. He was a specialist with the elderly and he gives help to incarnate souls who ask for it within his specialities."

"Are you saying that we all have access to others who have knowledge of a particular area of life that we don't?"

"That's right," she nodded, "and as a guide you have it too. I passed your request for help to someone more qualified to help you than me. So you see, Cherie, you are never left alone, there is always help if you ask for it."

Before he had a chance to ask any more questions, another voice behind him interjected.

"The Creator never asks something of you that is beyond your potential to achieve," Haniel said as she glided to their side on the fallen log, and Danielle smiled and nodded her agreement.

"How true" she said, softly.

Haniel looked at Ethan. "But sometimes you need persuading of that fact."

Ethan looked sheepish but had to agree, as he still wasn't at all certain he could measure up.

"So," Haniel said, "Ethan, I have been given permission to guide you on a special mission. You will be allowed to choose three people who, for different reasons, need special help at this time and bring them up to Heaven."

Danielle gasped and then clapped her hands in delight, though Ethan frowned and looked from one to the other. It was obvious from Danielle's reaction that this was a good thing yet he had no idea what it meant.

"Oh, Cherie, you are most fortunate."

Haniel nodded. "Yes you are, but let me explain what it's all about. This honour was once only the preserve of the archangels. We would hear the cries for help from Earth and sometimes the Creator allowed us to bring grace to a deeply troubled soul."

"Grace?" he queried, frowning again.

"Divine intervention, or grace as we call it, is a spiritual nudge in the right direction."

"Oh, I see," Ethan said, although he wasn't too sure that he did.

"Anyway," Haniel continued, "as the human population increased, more and more souls were interconnecting on a three-dimensional world, though angels have never been in the flesh. We do not know what it is like to be human, so it became harder for us to work very closely with you. It was decided that guides, who had been human, needed to be trained to help those still on the planet, which is what we have done now for millennia. But sometimes certain souls cry out for more than just guidance, they ask for divine intervention. Guides like Danielle can only pass on these requests, as they do not have the power or authority to grant such pleas, only the Creator can do that. And then we have people like you, Ethan."

"Like me?"

"Yes, guides in training who would benefit from experiencing helping others."

Ethan pursed his lips and felt that he ought to be going around with an L-plate pinned to his chest. Haniel's face twitched a little as the image appeared before her, but she also felt it was apt.

"The Creator proposed a solution to the problem of how to show you practically what a difference you can make without direct interference. It is a fine balancing act and one that needs a steady hand, but it is very rewarding and well worth the effort. Isn't that right, Danielle?"

She nodded, happily. "It is, Cherie, even if your charge is as difficult as you." Ethan raised an eyebrow at that last comment.

"So this chance I'm being given," he asked, "is like winning the lottery?

Haniel frowned. "What is a lottery?" she queried.

"It's when you buy a ticket and, if it is picked out, you win a big prize," he told her, but she shrugged.

"In a way it is a bit like that, yet it is a great honour to be given an opportunity to go to Heaven for a short period of time and to understand that life, death and rebirth is a natural cycle one should not fear. Or a chance to talk to a loved one who is in the spirit world, to sort out a problem that is preventing them carrying on with their own lives."

Ethan nodded as he began to get the idea, but he had more questions.

"I see," he said slowly. "It's like having a glimpse of Heaven then?" Haniel nodded so he then asked, "But how is that considered non-interference?" Danielle giggled at the question, as it was so typical of him, and Haniel decided to turn the tables on him.

"Why don't you tell me?"

Ethan snorted. "Aren't you supposed to be telling me?" he demanded, somewhat put out by Haniel's reversal. But Haniel wasn't upset, she just smiled.

"Do you not learn more by thinking it out for yourself?" she asked. "You are an intelligent being, and it's not that hard."

Ethan suppressed the desire to retort and, instead, kept his peace and turned his attention to coming up with the right answer. Once he put his mind to it, he found that Haniel was right again as it wasn't hard to see the difference.

"I guess you can take a horse to water but you can't make it drink," he said. Both Haniel and Danielle were momentarily stunned by his answer, but very soon they were laughing.

"Oh, my dear," Danielle spluttered between giggles, "that is so you, Cherie, so you."

"But you are correct too," Haniel added, "as you cannot make anyone learn anything. This opportunity is sometimes wasted, but all you will be allowed to do is give them that chance and then help if help is asked for."

"And how do I choose who should get this honour?" he queried.

"Honours," Haniel corrected. "You will be given three chances and you needn't worry about choosing the souls to give them to, for they will choose you." He frowned and was about to ask how when Haniel continued. "I know," she said, with just a hint of a smile on her exquisite face, "you now want to know how they'll do that. Well, it works like this. The Creator has received many requests for divine intervention and the ones where it is appropriate will be granted. Usually this is a task for archangels but, in this case, you have been chosen to perform it. You and I will tune into an area on

Earth where souls who are to receive grace reside and then the souls who will teach you the most will be the ones you connect with. It is a two-way street. You will help them but they will also help you with your understanding and confidence as well."

"The Creator is indeed all-knowing, compassionate and loving," Danielle said, humbly.

"The Creator is all that," Haniel replied, simply.

For once, Ethan had nothing to say as they sat together in reverent silence, contemplating the perfection of the Divine.

Ben sighed once more as he rubbed his temples trying to get rid of the pain inside his head, caused by his guilt and confusion. He was weary and he ached all over, so he got up and stretched out his six feet two frame as he tried to think rationally.

"Shouldn't I feel great?" he said, as he believed he had found love again. But he didn't. In fact, he only felt guilty, like he was betraying Karen and didn't deserve to be happy without her. Karen was dead and had been for several years but he still felt married to her and missed her wisdom and love.

"Oh, Karen, I wish I'd gone instead of you," he said to himself, feeling overwhelmed by life and all its complexities. He walked to the window and looked out over the garden they had planned and planted together, and remembered many happy days spent at garden centres buying plants and putting them into place in their grand plan. It had been so much fun. Now it was matured and looked wonderful but she wasn't here to enjoy it. He sighed and turned away, moving back to his desk. But he didn't feel like doing any more on the computer so turned it off.

He left his office, made a cup of coffee and took it into the garden where he sat on the wooden bench which was now showing its age; he'd not replaced it as it had been the first thing they'd bought for their new garden. He always felt closer to Karen when sitting on it and now he could really do with talking to her.

Ben knew that his friends thought he had got over her death and was ready to move on, but he wasn't so sure about that. He knew that at thirty-three he still had a lot of his life in front of him and if he said so himself he wasn't bad looking with his dark blond hair, blue eyes and tall, athletic build; but did he want to risk the pain of loving and losing again? He sighed as he couldn't answer that question, which made moving on so difficult.

It didn't help that others kept pressurising him to 'get on with his life', whatever that meant, and start dating again. He had resisted for as long as he could and begun to resent the well-meaning friends who invited him to dinner only to try to set him up with 'suitable woman'. He had been amazed at some of their choices for him and somewhat insulted. Then a new lady had joined the office and he had felt a stirring of interest in her; but then the guilt flooded him and now he didn't know what to do.

"Help me, Karen," he said. No-one replied, but someone was listening.

CHAPTER 3

A Cry for Help

Ethan found himself later that day walking to the Hall of the Graces, a place few guides go to; but as Ethan was now to choose someone in need, he had his own entry pass until the three gifts had been given. The building was round in shape and made of what looked like white marble, except that it was the brightest, most perfect marble imaginable. Ethan gazed at its brilliance in awe, taking in the fact that he couldn't see a single join in the stonework: it was perfectly smooth and seamless. It wasn't a large building, housing only one circular chamber in its interior, but it was still very impressive and reminded him of ancient Grecian temples with its evenly spaced, elegant, fluted columns all around. They were at the top of seven beautifully crafted, circular steps, which led up to the chamber inside. Haniel smiled at Ethan's face as he stared open-mouthed and wide-eyed at the edifice. She gave him a few moments to wonder at its perfection and glory before she gently touched his shoulder and said.

"It is time to begin, Ethan."

He nodded and together they began to ascend the stairs to the two massive, glowing doors of polished rose quartz crystal that sparkled with light and energy. He found it impossible to rationalise the beauty before him and the only word he found was, "Wow". Haniel nodded.

"Wow, indeed," she said, softly.

As they reached the top step, the doors began to open smoothly and effortlessly, without a sound, and Ethan trembled with both excitement and trepidation. He wasn't at all sure what he'd find inside as bright white light shone from the inner Hall of the Graces, so intense that it hurt his eyes to gaze upon it. He lifted one arm to shield his face and took Haniel's hand with the other, and with her to guide him he entered the inner sanctum, the place where Heaven and Earth meet. He had heard it called that but he didn't understand what it meant. He was about to find out. Once inside, the great doors gently closed behind them and the brilliance of the light slowly dimmed until he was able to see again. What he saw wasn't what he'd expected or imagined, as the round room was at first sight empty. Yet how could that be? He looked around him and the only thing he could see was a marble bench in one solid piece, forming a perfect circle in the centre of the interior. Ethan frowned and Haniel smiled at his confusion. She had brought many guides such as him here over the centuries and they all looked as he did, confused and a little disappointed, but she knew that he wouldn't be once he saw what was enclosed by the bench.

"Come with me," she said, leading him to the centre where he got his first sight of what lay beyond.

"Oh my," he stuttered, amazed at the sight below him, almost unable to comprehend what his eyes were showing him. There, in the floor, was Earth as he had seen it on the TV or films, as seen from space. It was so majestic, a blue and white jewel spinning slowly in a magenta void, with a halo of blue light surrounding it. He watched in fascination as it turned; he could pick out the continent of Australia, then an ocean, then India and South Africa before another huge ocean, until he saw the Americas.

Haniel watched it too. She never tired of its beauty and life yet, on such a wondrous world, there was such ugliness, violence and fear. To her, it was hard to understand why anyone would want to despoil such beauty. What did they get out of such disfigurement? Earth is a sentient, feeling being that gave so much and asked for so little in return, as all she wanted was to live in harmony with the life forms that occupied her. For the most part, she had. For millennia, the plants, animals and birds lived on her, taking only what they needed to survive and to procreate; even Man did this at first but then became greedy and began to believe that he owned the Earth and could do as he pleased with her. He forgot the wisdom of his ancestors who understood that everything must be balanced: what you take, you must balance with what you give.

"How can killing the only world you live on be considered progress?" she wondered aloud as she glanced at her student; he was still enthralled by the sight before them. But it was time for him to go to work. She touched his arm and motioned to him that they should take a seat and he nodded, still too overwhelmed to speak. They stepped over the marble bench and sat together; as they did so, the planet appeared to stop revolving and the continent of Europe was clearly defined below them.

"What's happening?" Ethan asked, concerned that the planet had stopped revolving. Haniel smiled.

"Do not worry, Ethan. Earth is still spinning, never fear. What is happening is that the Creator is showing you the place on Earth where He will grant the gifts of divine intervention."

Ethan frowned. "So, somewhere in Europe, I'll find three people to help?" he asked. She laughed.

"Oh, there are hundreds of people in Europe who could use your help," she said.

"Oh, great," he muttered under his breath, although she heard him quite clearly anyway.

"Don't be alarmed, Ethan, it is not so hard a task." The expression on his face showed her that he wasn't convinced, so she continued, "All you have to do is focus."

"Focus?" he asked.

"You must relax and allow your soul to tune in. Focus on the calling of Earthbound souls asking for help."

"And I'll be able to hear them?"

"Very clearly," she said.

"So, what do I do then?"

She smiled. These guides were so funny as they all expected to have to do something, yet it was just the opposite.

"You do nothing," she said, raising a hand to prevent him butting in, "except drop all of your preconceived ideas and just listen."

"Listen and that's it?" he stated indignantly.

"Just listen. I know it is a concept most people have forgotten but, for this to work, you must listen and, believe me, it'll be good practice for when you are a guide."

Ethan nodded slowly, remembering his little chat with Danielle. He had got the message quite clearly that guiding consisted of a lot of listening and he'd be the first to admit it wasn't something he was particularly good at, although they do say that 'practice makes perfect'.

"Okay. So, do I close my eyes?" he asked.

"If you want to."

He decided that he did and Haniel smiled as she watched his face. Like all those who had come before him, the look of deep concentration was soon etched on his features; the frown lines deepened as he tried harder and harder and heard less and less, until finally he opened his eyes.

"Nothing's happening," he wailed.

How she kept from laughing, Haniel did not know but, with her face straight, she said, "Because you are trying too hard."

"Oh!" he exclaimed and sighed again. "I get it. It's like meditation, the harder you try, the more you block it out."

She nodded. "That's right, so this time relax. Let go and drift and maybe keep your eyes open this time, take yourself into those clouds down there and go with the flow."

Ethan grinned as he never thought angels would use phrases like 'go with the flow' although it was good advice, so he decided to follow it. He gazed at the planet and let go of the need to do anything and, as the focus softened, he felt himself floating until, with a jerk, he came back into the chamber and looked surprised. Haniel sighed inwardly; he had nearly gone but something stopped him.

"What is the matter, Ethan?" she asked.

He blinked twice as he struggled for an answer and in the end all he could muster was a rather feeble, "I don't know." She smiled, ever patient.

"It is natural to be a little anxious at first but, remember, you are not in a physical body now, you cannot be hurt by the atmosphere or from falling. It is your spirit that is flying, not your former vehicle."

He nodded and did understand; he had felt that he was in his former body and, when he'd started to fall towards Earth, he couldn't help panicking.

"I'm sorry, I guess I forgot that," he said sheepishly.

"It is quite natural but unnecessary. You cannot die." She paused and let her words sink in then added, "Now, try again."

He nodded and once again looked down on Earth and let his mind drift. Slowly, he became aware that he had left the Hall of Graces and was floating. This time he didn't panic but relaxed and even began to enjoy the experience as it was pleasant just drifting gently down, peaceful and calming. On he went into the blackness of space, then inside the outer layer of Earth's atmosphere until he began to see the sky below him was lighter; and as soon as he registered this fact, he began to hear human voices. They were very faint at first, almost like whispers on the wind, but gradually, as he descended, they grew louder and louder until it became quite painful. He stopped, confused and not sure how to proceed. The cries for help were deafening.

"How will I ever find the right one to help amongst this appalling noise?" Ethan tried to clear his thoughts and a clear, calm voice came into his ear saying one word, "Focus", and he knew Haniel was still there to guide him. The feeling of panic subsided as he did as she said, deciding to say a little prayer to himself for support. 'Creator, I am your servant and I ask for your help to find the ones amongst the many whom you wish me to serve.'

As he finished his silent prayer, the volume of crying voices desisted and he could pick out a single female voice from the crowd. He had to listen hard to hear her words as they were faint, as if she were elderly or ill.

"Oh, God," she said, "I don't know what to do."

Ethan moved closer to where the voice originated from and found himself floating above a small H-shaped building, the centre spar of which was roofed in glass panels. He frowned and wondered what this place was until, in a flash, he knew all he needed to know, given to him in a heartbeat. This was a nursing home and the voice was one of the patients. He moved closer again, passing effortlessly through the roof and drifting down the glassed corridor that connected four units, each consisting of six bedrooms, a lounge, dining area and small kitchen. It was well maintained and appeared a happy place, even though he knew none of the twenty-four residents would ever leave it except to return to the spirit world. There were plants and seats in this corridor area where patients and their relatives were enjoying the light and airiness of the space that made it well used.

But the one he was seeking wasn't there, so he moved on into one of the units off the corridor. He passed through the small lounge and kitchen to the bedrooms beyond and it took him no time at all to find the right door; on it he read 'Mrs Kathleen O'Connor'. He continued on into her room and found an elderly man sitting next to the bed in which a very frail, grey-haired lady lay. Ethan took a few seconds to study them and, as he did so, he realised that the body in the bed did not contain much of the woman's spirit anymore.

"This is not right," he said, frowning, and was surprised when the frail voice he'd been tracking spoke to him.

"Who's there?" it asked hesitantly.

He looked around to locate the source, when he spotted cloudy energy floating some feet above the small fragile body on the bed. It was then he knew that the spirit of Kathleen had almost left the physical plane for good but, for some reason, she was hanging on almost in a state of limbo, neither dead nor alive. Why this was, he didn't know nor understand but he was going to find out.

"Hello, Kathleen. Don't be afraid, I won't hurt you."

There was a pause before she replied, "Where are you?"

"I'm here, right next to you," he said, and moved to the side of her shadowy form to reassure her.

"I can't see you," the voice said with a note of panic in it.

"Don't look for me with your eyes, Kathleen. Look for me with your heart." There was a pause before he added, "Do you understand?"

"Yes, yes I do," she whispered and, as soon as she stopped trying, she began to discern a shape, wispy and indistinct at first, floating not far from her. "Is that you?" she asked in an uncertain voice.

"Yes, Kathleen, it is me."

"Are you an angel?" she wondered, half in awe of this form that was now more recognisable as a human-like being.

"No, I'm not, but I have been sent by them to help you."

"Help me? Why?"

"Because you've asked for it," Ethan replied, in surprise.

"Oh!" she exclaimed. "Really?"

Ethan sighed again as this wasn't turning out quite as he had envisaged.

"Yes, really," he said, wearily. "And I am here," he told her. Now she could suddenly see him like a misty cloud, slowly forming into a human shape until she could see Ethan quite clearly. He wasn't an angel, but his face was young and angelic, if a little disappointing; he looked wan and for some reason that upset her, as she felt that she was the cause of his sadness. She didn't like to upset anyone.

"Thank you for coming," she said. "Do you have a name, dear?"

"Yes, I'm Ethan. And before you ask, I'm a guide."

"A guide?" she frowned. "For whom? Me?"

Ethan didn't quite know how to explain what his job was or whether he should admit that he was still only in training; it might be self-defeating if he told her his true status. After all, if he were going to help her, she'd have to believe he could even if he was having doubts himself. He knew he had to say something, so he took the plunge.

"No, I'm not your guide but you do have one, or more than one, and they've been with you all your life. Have you made contact with them?"

She wasn't sure about that, but there had been times when she'd thought she heard a small voice offering advice; whenever she had listened, things had worked out all right. But was that guidance or something else? He heard her thoughts and smiled.

"No, that was your guide," he said. She looked across at him in surprise.

"You know what I'm thinking?" she asked. Ethan nodded.

"Yes I do, though even I'm not sure how. I've learned it's better not to ask questions like that. The main thing is that I'm here to help you with whatever it is you asked God for."

She looked at him with an expression of expectation, intermingled with puzzlement. She wasn't too sure of what she wanted, except that she knew the situation she and her beloved husband, Frank, were in couldn't continue. But what to do? That was the question she needed help with.

As quickly as Kathleen was thinking this, Ethan perceived detailed pictures of the O'Connors' lives and understood their predicament. He absorbed this information instantly and knew that Haniel was giving him a much needed helping hand; so now it was up to him. What he felt most strongly was Kathleen's fear; she was scared to let go of her Earthly life even though the ravages of Alzheimer's had reduced her body to little more than a useless shell. What made it all so much worse was that although she could no longer communicate anything to anyone, she could still see Frank's distress and knew that he felt such conflicting emotions. He loved her deeply, she knew, and he wanted her to stay with him but not in this state. Day after day, she lay looking up at the ceiling, her limbs twisted into contorted positions, unmoving and unable to communicate, and it broke his heart.

CHAPTER 4

A Day Trip to Heaven

For the past five years since the fateful day that the MRI scan revealed she was a victim of Alzheimer's, he had had to watch her disappear before his eyes. It had been slow at first, with the help of the drugs, but eventually even they couldn't halt the relentless advance of this most devastating disease. Bit by bit, she changed from the vivacious, witty and clever woman in whom he'd fallen in love to a confused, frustrated and destructive being who couldn't understand what was happening to her. After two exhausting years of trying to cope on his own, the time came when he knew it would be in Kathleen's best interest to move into a care home, where she could get full-time care and attention. It had been a difficult decision, but he couldn't cope with her following him around twenty-four hours a day or her fits of temper and the lack of sleep he suffered when she began to get up in the night, convinced it was morning. One day he had nearly hit her, which shocked him, but there was no escape from her and her constant talking; it was like Chinese torture, one drip at a time until he couldn't take any more.

He was so tired and yet he couldn't rest or relax with her in the house, worried what she might do next. If he didn't lock the outside doors, she would get out and wander into the neighbours' gardens or even into their houses. Luckily, they were very understanding when he apologised and explained her condition but it was still a nightmare for him when she vanished. The postman brought her home one day and the milkman found her on another. So he had to keep everything locked, which made him feel even more trapped and isolated. Finally, his own health began to fail him and the decision was made. Kathleen was assessed at the local hospital's special unit for a week before, by a stroke of good luck, a bed at the small specialist home called Home Fields became available and she was moved. Places were few and far between for people with Alzheimer's as they are so difficult to manage, but a place had freed up just when Kathleen needed it. Frank knew how fortunate they were.

Now, three years later, there was hardly a day when he didn't drive the ten minutes to be by her side, even if she didn't appear to know who he was or why he came. Kathleen looked across at him as he picked up her limp hand and placed it on his wet cheek. He too had changed with age and the strain of her illness, which had bent his back, and his once handsome face was now thin and bony. He had more grey in his dark hair but it was still thick as it used to be. How she had loved to run her fingers threw that mane of his.

"Kathleen, oh my darling, I wish you could hear me."

She sighed and looked away. "I can, my love, I can," she said sadly, but he couldn't hear her.

Ethan winced as the pain he felt in each of them was sharp and raw but, on the Earthly plane, there was no way it could change. The damage to Kathleen's brain couldn't be repaired but, if he could persuade her to let go of her body and ascend to Heaven, he knew that both of them would have a chance to heal. The open wound would close in time and, if they wished, they would be reunited in the next world, a place of exquisite beauty, love and compassion where pain no longer exists.

He suddenly knew what he was here for: to give Kathleen a chance to see and experience its love for herself, so that the fear that kept her tied to her fading physical vehicle would disappear and she could be free. In freeing herself, she would also free her husband and their children from the suffering they were experiencing, as they could do nothing to help her now, only watch her die inch by inch and agonisingly slowly. Ethan looked at her and, as he tried to find the right words to persuade her to come with him, he felt the golden light of the angels fall upon him and the words began to flow.

"Kathleen, I know you believe in Heaven and have lived a good life. On your path, your kindness and gentleness have helped many, and even those whom you met only once have been touched by you." She turned her head to look at him, a surprised look in her faded, blue eyes.

"Is that true?" she whispered. Ethan nodded.

"Yes, it is true. Now it is time you received help for yourself."

"I just want to help Frank," she said, smiling. "You help him, dear, I'm alright." But Ethan shook his head.

"No, Kathleen, to help Frank you have to help yourself. You fear death greatly and it's this fear that is binding you to Earth. You know what I am telling you is the truth."

She sighed and nodded although she didn't want to admit that he was right; yet she didn't know why she had this dread in her heart. All her life, she'd been a practising Christian and believed in Heaven and Hell, as the priests had told her. Suddenly a face came to mind and she shuddered. It was a face from the distant past, when she'd been a child living in a small rural town in Ireland, the face of the Catholic priest, Father Michael, who preached pure fire and brimstone, relishing in what the devil did to naughty children and the fires that would consume them. He'd yelled at the congregation, his long, equine face contorted in delight as he spewed forth his words of death and darkness. Once, he'd pointed his long, bony finger at her and said:

" ...and your soul will be cursed to everlasting pain and despair in the fires of Hell for your sins. Death will not end your suffering - it is only the beginning of eternal damnation."

Ethan heard those words clearly as she remembered them and began to understand why she feared death so much.

"Kathleen, Father Michael was wrong," he said, softly. She was startled by his words, as much by what he said as to how he knew about Father Michael.

"Wrong? What do you mean, dear?" she whispered.

"There is no such Hell, Kathleen. God isn't a revengeful being. He is full of love and light and he wants us to be happy, not sad. A being of pure love could never create Hell." She wasn't sure she believed him yet part of her wanted to.

"Are you saying there is no place called Hell?" she queried.

"No, I didn't quite say that. What I said was that God didn't create it - we did." She frowned, as he'd lost her completely now.

"You'll have to be clearer than that, dear," she said. "I don't know what you're on about."

Ethan sighed. This Helping People lark was harder work than he could ever have imagined. It wasn't just like a lottery where you find the lucky winner, handing over the prize and leave them to it. Oh no, there was a whole heap of hard graft attached to it, even to get the recipient to accept your help. He was beginning to think he'd been well and truly suckered and, quite frankly, he hadn't believed angels did that! A small but definite sound of someone laughing filtered through to him from somewhere. Well, he had accepted the offer of learning and enlightenment and he wasn't going to back out now. The only way was forward, so he gathered himself together to explain to Kathleen what Hell really was.

"Okay Kathleen, let me tell you about this place called Hell. When people graduate - that's what we call dying - they can choose where they want to go in the spiritual realms. You can do anything - make music, paint, learn new skills and meet old friends, whatever you want. Now, most people do this but there are a few who feel they should be punished for what they did while on Earth and believe they will go to Hell. But thoughts can become realities and, over the millennia, people's thoughts have created a place that they believe Hell should be like. But it's solely a creation of people's minds and it only exists because they want it to - they could leave at any time and enjoy the beauty, peace and love that is all around them, but they choose not to. So you see, Kathleen, you can go to Hell if you want to, but you'll not be sent there." She was speechless for a moment or two.

"But why would anyone want to?"

"I have no idea," Ethan shrugged, as the thought of condemning yourself to such a place was unimaginable to him, especially when you could be in paradise.

"So you're saying that if I believe I'll go to Hell, I could think myself there."

"You could," he agreed, "but you won't because you are much too sensible a person to buy into such nonsense." For a second her face went blank then she realised what he'd said and a beautiful smile slowly crept across her features, transforming them.

"You are right, my dear, I won't," she said, softly.

"Good. And now we've got that sorted out, perhaps you'd like to have a little trip."

"A trip?"

"Yes, a look at what really happens when you die, like a day trip to Heaven," he said, mischievously. Now he'd got her attention and was rewarded by the stunned expression that appeared on her face. She stared open-mouthed at him until finally she regained her wits.

"Don't you have to die to go to Heaven?"

"Normally, yes, but I can show you what is waiting for you there by visiting just for a short while so you won't be afraid."

"You mean, I can go with you to Heaven but I will still be alive?" She was frowning now.

Ethan didn't think her physical body was very alive; he certainly wouldn't want to come back to it, as it lay here day after day, immobile and unresponsive. To him, that was a fate much worse than death but then he did already know that a better place was waiting for him. His own passing had been swift and peaceful – despite the trauma - and now, if he could show Kathleen what was 'on the other side' maybe she could pass over peacefully and happily too.

"Yes, Kathleen, your body will still be here waiting for you. You are still connected to it." He pointed down and, as she followed his finger, she noticed for the first time the silver cord that was attached to her stomach and seemed to come out of the physical body in the same place.

"Oh, my!" she exclaimed and reached out to touch it, to see if it was real. Her hand seemed to go right through it and she gasped in astonishment; Ethan had to smother a laugh as he watched her.

"It's okay, it's real. But you are in your light body and that isn't solid like a physical body. In this dimension, you are as light as a snowflake and can pass through doors, roofs and walls as easily as blinking."

"But I'm still attached to my physical one, down there." She looked down at her small, fragile form in the large bed below.

"Don't worry, the cord will stretch as far as you need to go. It won't break," he said, reassuringly. "You are the one who decides when you want to let go."

"I do?"

"Yep, you do. Though it's not much of a life like that is it?" he added, suddenly realising that maybe he shouldn't have. She looked at herself and the ever patient Frank, and couldn't come up with any argument to contradict him. The only reason why she was still alive, she realised, was that she was too frightened to leave. Finally, she understood that her prayers were being answered, except not in the way she could ever have imagined. She smiled at Ethan.

"You are the answer to my prayers."

"I guess I am," he smiled back.

Kathleen knew that she wanted to take up Ethan's offer and as she accepted his outstretched hand, with a look back at her beloved husband, she felt positive for the first time in many years and there was hope in her face.

"Let's go," she said.

"Okay, hold tight."

They began to move upwards, straight through the ceiling and roof into the darkened skies beyond. Kathleen grinned at her guide, finding the experience of flying exhilarating. On they went, up and up through clouds and into the black inky stillness that was filled with stars, far more than can ever be seen from Earth.

"Oh, it's so beautiful," she whispered.

"Isn't it?" Ethan agreed, as they paused to absorb the glories of the universe all around them before they went on further. They entered a cyclical vortex that had appeared and there, a long way on, was a bright light at the end of it.

"Is this the tunnel to Heaven?" Kathleen asked. "I never thought it really existed."

"When we get to the light," said Ethan, "you'll be there."

The brightness would have been too painful to bear for physical eyes but, in her light body, Kathleen could look directly into it; at first she believed it was just a very brilliant, white light but slowly she began to see all the colours of the rainbow inside of it.

"Oh," she whispered, in awe at how incredibly beautiful those delicate, almost fragile colours were and how they shimmered and sparkled; there was nothing to compare it with on Earth, nothing close to its magical brilliance.

Ethan, who had seen the light many times, still marvelled at it as they got closer to the end of the tunnel, then suddenly they were surrounded by the light, immersed in its purity and love. Kathleen sighed. There was so much love here and she had never felt such compassion and empathy all around her. There was unearthly music too somewhere - or was it everywhere? - and the sound of joyful voices faintly rose and fell in perfect harmony. It was as if a Heavenly choir were practising and they were privileged to hear it. Ethan came to rest on his feet and Kathleen landed next to him; from the look of awestruck wonder on her face, he didn't need to ask if she were all right as he could see that the magic of Heaven was already working. He had been told by his own teachers that most souls only needed the shortest of visits to remember what they were missing and sometimes it was quite difficult to persuade those who still had much left to accomplish on Earth to return there after they had had a near-death experience. What they all took back with them was the love and beauty that had surrounded them and they were no longer afraid of dying. They now knew it was as painless as going from one room to another, taking off the physical body as easily as one would remove a coat; and, once there, loving beings were ready to greet one. So it was for Kathleen. Out of the light came two light forms, a man and a woman of about thirty-five years in appearance, and when Kathleen saw them she gasped.

"It can't be," she uttered.

"Yes it can, Kathleen," he replied, smiling, as her parents came forward to meet her. She had almost not recognised them as they were radiant and smiling, their faces unlined and untroubled, quite unlike how they had appeared in their Earthly life. Her mother held out a hand.

"Kathleen, my child," she said, her voice soft and full of love. "Come with us and let us tell you the truth."

CHAPTER 5

Judgement

Kathleen wasn't sure if she should go to them as they were so different from the rather grim-faced people she remembered. Her father stepped towards her and she found herself inadvertently backing away from him as he had always been a very intimidating man, pious and a strict disciplinarian. He had scared her, although he wasn't a violent man, but now he looked carefree and much more handsome without those deep worry lines.

"I understand," he said and smiled. "I scared you with my heaviness and I can only apologise, Kathleen. I believed I had to be strict so that you wouldn't dare get into any trouble. But I have seen the error of my ways and I know I should have trusted you and showed you how much I loved you. Instead of that, I lost you all too soon."

She knew what he meant, as she had met and married Frank when she was only eighteen, partly to escape from the family home. She had been fortunate that she had chosen a good and lovely man, whose love, even under the most trying of circumstances, had never faltered. It could have turned out so differently, with her jumping from the frying pan into the fire, yet now for the first time in her life she felt her father's love. It was like a warm wave, a blanket of deep peace and security; there was strength there but empathy and compassion too. She looked him in the face and saw all she had ever hoped for reflected back in his eyes; he did love her and it was quite a shock to realise how much he did and what that love felt like.

"Oh!" she exclaimed in surprise and it gave rise to a question she had always wanted to ask him but would never have dared to when he was alive. "Was I a disappointment to you?" she asked. Both her parents looked at each other in surprise.

"Never," her father said emphatically.

"No, Kathleen, you were our joy. Why would you think otherwise?" her mother asked.

"I just felt I didn't quite measure up to your expectations. I knew you wanted me to study for more qualifications but I just couldn't - it wasn't for me and I knew you were disappointed." Her father nodded.

"Yes, we were, but not because we felt you had let us down. It was because we wanted you to have the best chance to live a happy life. We thought that to be happy you needed money and to get money you needed qualifications and a good job. But now we see that it's not so - there are plenty of rich, unhappy people in the world. So, no Kathleen, we wanted you to be happy and we worried that, as young as you were when you married Frank, you might regret it later."

"But I never did. He is a wonderful man." They smiled and nodded.

"Yes, we know. You have been blessed, my child," her mother said.

Ethan had watched them and seen the green glow of healing that surrounded them. It was good that they'd had this time to start the healing process but their time in Heaven was limited because she was still attached to her physical form. So he'd have to move the proceedings along as there was something else very important he knew he had to show her. He coughed politely and they all looked at him as if they had forgotten he was there. He smiled.

"Kathleen, we must move on. Your parents will be here to meet you when you decide to let go of your body."

"Yes, we will, never fear. We are always close by," her mother said.

Kathleen swallowed hard as they moved off into the white mists and vanished and it was harder than she would have thought, seeing them leave again. Ethan gave her a few moments to compose herself before he continued.

"There is one other area that I knew you are fearful of." She frowned, unable to think what that was. "Judgement," he said. That one word was the power to make her afraid.

"Yes," she whispered. "I'm afraid of the judgement I shall receive."

"But no one judges you, Kathleen. Only you can do that."

She wasn't sure she'd heard him right, as hadn't the priests always said she would be judged when she got to Heaven? If she were found wanting, her soul would pay the price but now Ethan was saying differently.

"I judge me?" she queried. He nodded.

"That's right," he said, though the look on her face told him that just telling her the facts wasn't going to cut it. She needed to believe. "I know you don't believe me, so I'm going to show you." And, with that, they found themselves floating above four individuals in a circular room below.

"Where are we?" Kathleen asked.

"In the Halls of Reviewing," Ethan replied.

"Reviewing? Reviewing what?"

Ethan smiled. "Your last life. And once you have, you can decide what else you need to experience and what lessons need to be learned the next time you incarnate."

"And this is the judgement the priest talked about?" She frowned. It didn't appear to be at all threatening or intimidating as she had always imagined it would be, but Ethan shook his head.

"No, this is not at all like your priest said. The Church has been trying to control people for two thousand years and, when people were simple and uneducated, they could. But times change,

Kathleen, and once people could read the Bible for themselves they began to ask awkward questions. Some priests would try to frighten people into believing them, only it doesn't work like that as everyone is welcome here. As I told you before, only you can put yourself in Hell."

"So what about murderers, are they allowed in?"

"Yes, of course they are. But when they do their life review they will be faced with their wrong-doing and realise that they have to atone for it, which could take many lifetimes to achieve." He paused then added, "Have you heard of karma?"

"Karma? Is that a curry, dear?" she asked, frowning. Ethan burst out laughing and it took a few moments for him to stop.

"Oh, Kathleen, that's a classic. I must remember that one." He smiled broadly. "No, it's not curry. Karma is a universal law."

"A law? Do you mean God's law?"

"Yes, it's the Creator's law. The easiest way to understand it is 'you reap what you sow'." Kathleen nodded, very familiar with her Bible, but Ethan wasn't so sure she really understood what it meant. "So, what do you think it means?" She paused and had a little think before she replied.

"That if you hurt someone, someone will hurt you."

"That's the simplistic version, but it's much more complex than that. You see, over many lifetimes, karma between individuals builds up but you don't necessarily pay back one person with the karma you owe them. You may pay back someone else – the debt will still have been paid." He saw her looking a little confused and didn't blame her as it was confusing, although perfect in its execution. The Creator knew what He was doing and souls grow with each experience. "I know it's a bit of a struggle to understand how it all works out but, believe me, it does."

"I'm sure it does," she nodded, "and it's not my place to question God."

"No, I suppose it isn't. Still, everyone pays the karmic price for their actions. No-one escapes, but none are condemned."

"Yes, I see." She looked down again at the people below and

asked, "So, what's happening here? Who are these people?" Ethan looked down.

"This is a life review and the three in the triangle are the Trine," he said.

"The Trine?"

"Yes, you know your Bible, Kathleen, so who do you think they are?" he replied, turning her question back to her to answer. She frowned, then a thought came to her.

"They're not the Holy Trinity, are they?"

"In a way they are, but we call them the Trine, as their race helps all who are ready to review their lives, whatever religion they may have followed on Earth."

"Their race? Are there more then?" Her face showed her surprise.

"Yes, they are a sort of angel, a separate sub-group if you like, whose purpose is to help the souls who incarnate to understand their last life so they can plan the next one."

"So they're judges."

"No-one judges anyone, Kathleen, they assist."

"How?"

He looked down on the unfolding scene below them.

"Watch and you'll see," he said.

The man who stood in the middle of the room was middle-aged and portly with receding, sandy hair and freckled skin; his attitude was belligerent and arrogant even in the company of the Trine. Kathleen frowned.

"He doesn't seem ready to review his life to me."

Ethan agreed but he knew the rules.

"No, he doesn't, but he thinks he is, so the Trine is here to help him." He paused. "Although I don't think he's going to enjoy the experience very much."

"What do you mean?"

Ethan grinned at her. "Once you've decided that you're ready for a life review, there's no going back. It takes place and continues until all issues are resolved, regardless of how difficult it is. I just want you to understand that no-one judges you except you yourself and then you decide how to make amends. There is no-one pushing you or making you do anything you don't want to do. Believe me, once you've gone through this process, you understand so much more and can see so much more clearly that you are grateful and only too happy to start planning the next trip to Earth."

"He doesn't look grateful," Kathleen said, pointing to the man.

"No, but it is hard to face your faults and admit you could have done so much better - all those wasted opportunities."

They both listened in to what was being said. It was only then that Kathleen noticed that one of the sides of the triangle linking the three white-robed figures of the Trine was, in fact, a screen of some sort; she focused on it and saw flashes of scenes, some of which included the man in them.

"What are they watching?"

"It is a fast-forward of his life, a bit like a movie, only this is what really happened and not what we like to think happened."

"The truth and nothing but the truth," she whispered. Ethan nodded.

"In glorious technicolour."

It became clear that the man had been a doctor on Earth and he was very proud of that, looking down on others whom he judged as not doing as well as he had. As this was shown, he at first made excuses but gradually, as more and more instalments were revealed and the pattern firmly established, he had to admit it was true. Then he was shown what he missed when he judged others as inferior: the good friends he could have had, the interesting person his neighbour was and the missed opportunities that would have embellished his life. The puffed-up, arrogant man began to deflate as he realised just how narrow-minded he had become and how his career had taken over his life to the extent that his family never saw him.

"But I provided for them," he pleaded and it was acknowledged that, materially, they wanted for nothing; but emotional support and love had been sorely lacking. On the screen, he saw his children discussing him and was shocked to hear them say they both would rather have had fewer presents and more time with him; they remembered how many times he'd broken his promises about taking them to a ball game or going on a family picnic. Even holidays were fitted around his schedule and subject to change or even cancellation.

"But I loved them," he said, sadly.

"Yes but did you show them you did?"

"No, I suppose I thought they knew," he admitted, shaking his head.

"So, what is important?"

He looked up, his face miserable and somewhat ashamed. "Love and caring," he said, sadly.

"Hear, hear," Ethan added softly, turning to her Kathleen.

"Now, do you understand?"

"Yes, I think I do, but what happens to him now?"

"Oh, that's just the start. But he'll be fine and when it's all over he'll be given a new guide and lots of help mapping out what he'd like to achieve next time."

"Will he go back straight away?"

"That depends on a lot of things. He might decide to wait for one or more of those he was with to graduate, then they could reincarnate together, if that's appropriate. Or he could go back fairly soon, or in a hundred years' time. But it will be when the time is right for his soul to experience what it needs, to evolve and grow."

"I see. So, every time we incarnate, it isn't just random. We've planned it out before we start."

"Yep," he said, knowing what she was going to ask next as he had asked the same question himself.

"Then why do we make such a mess of it?"

Ethan laughed. He had often wondered that.

"I know, it seems strange, doesn't it? But the reason is that once we are born we forget the plans we've made and most of us spend the rest of our lives trying to find out why we were born in the first place."

"Crazy," she said, softly.

He nodded, half of him agreeing with her, although he now understood why it was so.

"Yes, it is a bit. But remember, if we knew how our lives should be, like what career was right for us, where to live and who to marry, then it would be a very unchallenging and boring life. And we wouldn't be using free will."

"Yes, I suppose," she replied, grudgingly.

"So, instead, we have to work at it and, if we can work on our spiritual side, we have far more chance of connecting with our higher selves where the information we need is stored. And once we can do that, we find out what we had planned and can start working on it."

"And do many people succeed?"

"More and more every year, although I know it doesn't look like it from the surface. But things are changing on Earth and many people are becoming aware of their spiritual side and taking control of their lives."

She thought about that for a few moments and had to agree, having noticed more books on the spiritual way of life, both fiction and non-fiction, being published in the last decade or so. She herself had started to take yoga classes and especially enjoyed the meditation they did at the end of each one. The old religions were failing because they were built on fear and control, whereas the New Age, at its best, was built on love, responsibility and compassion. There were still people who tried to make money out of people's hopes and fears but, as the number of spiritual people in the world increased, the less likely they were to succeed.

Ethan knew that an exciting time to be on Earth was about to begin and he was being prepared to guide a soul who would take on the challenges ahead; as a guide, he'd have to help his charge with all of the problems they would face until the change occurred. What would happen then, he wasn't sure. But it would herald a new golden age for the whole planet. Still, this was for the future and now he had someone else to help.

CHAPTER 6

Angels are Always Right

"Kathleen, soon we will have to return to Earth." She nodded and sighed.

"I know, but it is so lovely here," she said as they walked on past beautiful buildings that seem to glow in this strange gold-tinted light that surrounded them. He smiled as he led her towards a particular building that he knew she would love to see for herself, although they would not have time to go inside now. But she could visit it when she returned for good. They walked on side by side, just taking in the sights and smiling at the other people they met along the way. They were all dressed so differently that she had to ask him:

"Ethan, is there a dress code up here?" For a second he was so surprised that he didn't answer and then he threw back his head and laughed.

"No, Kathleen," he finally managed to say. "Here you decide how and what you want to wear and it appears." She looked at him as if he were lying. "Honestly Kathleen, it does!"

"I believe you." She smiled slowly. "It saves on shopping then."

"Yes, but you can do that too if you want to. Everything is possible here - you can work, write music, paint and even cook if that's what you feel like doing. You can study anything - and this is where you might like to go to do that," he said as they arrived at a classical Greek building with impressive golden doors. Kathleen looked at it with a frown on her face and pointed to the lettering above the portico.

"What does that say?" she asked. Ethan sighed inwardly as he wasn't sure exactly; his ancient Greek was non-existent.

"This is the great library of Alexander the Great," he told her. She smiled, as it had always fascinated her for some reason and she had often wondered what wonderful books had been destroyed so long ago. This time she didn't doubt him and knew it was one place she would definitely be returning to. But now she looked at Ethan, knowing it was time for her to leave, at least for a short while, and felt reluctant to do it. It was only her love for Frank that was now compelling her to go back. Ethan knew what she was thinking.

"Yes, it is time. But you don't have to stay in your body - you can leave it at any time."

She knew that now but there was someone else to consider.

"But what about Frank?" she asked. "He'll be devastated if I leave him."

Ethan looked at her and understood her reluctance to leave such a kind, loving man. "He'll grieve, but he will be okay. You have two fine daughters who will look after him and gradually he will find enjoyment again." She looked a bit put out at that and he laughed. "Yes he will, Kathleen, and do you begrudge him that?" She had to think about that for a few seconds.

"No, of course I want him to be happy. I'm just being selfish."

"You're being human," Ethan replied. She smiled at that and didn't feel so bad. "Your husband is tied to your bedside. Day after day, he sits there and prays for you to be set free." Kathleen started in surprise.

"He does?" she exclaimed.

"Follow me and I'll show you."

They moved off into the white mist and she became aware of them descending. It didn't take any time at all before they were back, looking down on her frail body in a large bed with Frank sitting beside her, holding her hand and bending forward. They hovered above watching the scene and Kathleen was about to ask a question but Ethan put a finger to his lips, which stopped her. Instead, he pointed at Frank.

"Look."

Kathleen turned and studied him. At first, she didn't see anything out of the ordinary until his shoulders moved and she realised he was crying.

"Oh, Frank," she said sadly, wishing she could go to his side and wipe away the tears she could now see running down his face and noticing how old he looked now. Ethan knew this would be very difficult for her to witness, but if she believed that by staying she was helping Frank, she was deluding herself; in fact, he was suffering greatly, as were her daughters and their children. In cases like hers, it's the families who suffer the most, watching their loved one disappear and being unable to do anything to stop it, until finally there is no-one at home and the eyes are just blank canvases, empty of emotion and life. Frank lifted her hand to his lips and kissed it. Ethan motioned that they should move closer, which they did. Kathleen could smell his aftershave and touched his hair lightly with her ethereal hand. Frank looked around as he felt their presence behind him but he didn't see them, their vibrations being too fast for human eyes to capture, so he frowned and turned back, bending forward to talk to the body in the bed.

"Kathleen, I don't know if you can hear me or even understand what I'm saying."

She smiled sadly and said, "Oh, I can, my love, I can."

Frank sighed and continued. "Anyway, even if you can't hear me, I have to tell you how I feel." He paused again to try and arrange his thoughts coherently. "Does it matter? You probably can't hear me anyway, but I love you, Kathleen. I fell in love with you the first time I saw you, remember that? You were walking home with your sister Mary, and I was with Bernard. I was so tongue-tied, I couldn't say anything and felt such a fool, and it took me a long time to pluck up the courage to ask you out. I couldn't believe it when you said 'Yes'." He smiled at the memory and shook his head as if he still couldn't believe it.

"You were the most beautiful girl in all of Kerry, going out with the likes of me. I was the most envied man around and I felt like a king. I walked taller because of you, Kathleen." He patted her hand. "You made me, my love. Without your love and encouragement, I'd never have amounted to much and I'd never have dared to leave Ireland and follow my dreams. No, I'd probably never have left the building sites like the one I was working on when we met. I can still remember your words to me when I told you how I dreamed of being an architect. Can you remember that?"

He looked down at her face but it remained blank, her blue eyes fixed on the ceiling and he wondered if it was worth carrying on. But somehow he felt better airing his thoughts out loud and maybe, just maybe, she was listening, so he continued.

"You said, 'If there is any way you can fulfil your dream, Frank, you must do it.' I did, even though you were brave enough to marry me before I left to get my qualifications so I could support you like you deserved." He smiled. "And how beautiful you were on our wedding day. You shone like an angel - my angel. Was that really over forty years ago? It seems like yesterday." He lifted her hand to his cheek as the tears began to flow again. "You are so precious to me but I can't bear to see you like this and know it will only get worse. You know I love you and will never stop loving you but, Kathleen, it's time for you to be free."

Kathleen looked at Ethan in surprise. "He wants me to die?" she asked. Ethan shook his head.

"Not really, but he knows what the future will bring if you stay. He will have to witness you starving to death and not be able to do anything about it."

"Starve to death?" she repeated, frowning, unsure she'd heard him right.

"Yes, that's what I said. Frank knows all about Alzheimer's now and you have entered the last stages. In the end, you'll not be able to swallow any more as it's the last reflex to go and you will starve to death."

She shuddered and made a face. "That's horrible."

"Yes it is, but it happens," Ethan agreed.

"But dogs are treated better than that," she said, indignantly.

"Yes, they are. It's a sad reflection on the human race that we give our pets more dignity than our fellow humans."

She nodded and sighed. "So, Frank wants me to leave?"

"In a way. He knows you can't be cured and the alternative would be too awful for him and your girls to bear."

She finally understood and with that understanding came a sense of relief and lightness. "Then I'm free to leave?"

"Yes, you can go back to Heaven any time you want to."

She looked back at Frank and then upwards as if to Heaven, and made her decision. "Then I'll go," she said softly.

"If that's what you want. It is your decision," he said.

"I know. But I'd like to say goodbye to him if I can."

Ethan wasn't sure how she could do that. But he needn't have worried as someone more senior did; in an instant, an angelic presence surrounded them and the archangel Haniel was with them. She had conjured up the image of wings for Kathleen and had them outstretched, making her an awesome sight, and from the look on Kathleen's face she was suitably impressed.

"An angel," she breathed.

"Oh, yes, this is Haniel," Ethan smiled.

Kathleen didn't quite know what to say to an angel, so she smiled and stayed silent. Haniel looked at her student.

"Well, Ethan, you see that you can help people if you put your mind to it." Ethan sighed, knowing that he was getting a gentle rebuke even now. Haniel smiled at him then turned her attention to Kathleen.

"We are pleased that you have decided to leave the Earth at this time. You have nothing to fear as many are waiting to greet you on the other side."

Kathleen nodded. "I know, and I'm ready. But if possible, can I say goodbye to Frank?"

Haniel smiled. "It is an honour to grant such a wish," she replied. "Just lay your form over your physical body and think yourself inside. Once there, say your goodbye then rise again and your parents will be here to guide you home."

Kathleen nodded and turned to Ethan. "Thank you, Ethan, for your help."

"It's been a pleasure, Kathleen," he replied. As he spoke, he realised that it had been, even if at times he'd felt well out of his depth. He had coped though and in coping had himself grown. He supposed that was the point, wasn't it?

Kathleen looked at her body and moved towards it. Haniel had made it all sound so simple but she wondered if it would it prove to be. 'Only one way to find out', she said to herself as she lay down her etheric form over her physical one; one last look at Haniel and slowly she felt herself sinking and getting heavier and heavier. It was like being dragged down by mud, sucked inside an old, worn-out shell that had lost its ability to move at all unaided and she didn't like it at all; but it would be worth it to see Frank and touch him one last time. Her physical body shuddered as she re-entered it and she could see out of her eyes once more. Frank was jolted out of his memories by her sudden and unexpected movement. She blinked a couple of times and, with some difficulty, turned her head to face him. His eyes opened wider in surprise as, for once, there was life and intelligence registering in her beautiful blue eyes.

"Kathleen, can you hear me?" he asked anxiously, wondering if he were maybe imagining this after hoping so long for one last spark of recognition from her. She smiled.

"Yes, Frank, always."

He burst into tears and held her hand but she didn't have long, so she spoke again.

"I love you, Frank, but it's time for me..." She struggled with her words after being silent for over a year; it was as if her mouth had forgotten how to work. "...time for me to go now. Goodbye, my love."

He brushed the tears from his eyes. "Goodbye, Kathleen, until we meet again." He leaned forward and kissed her gently on the lips and with that she sighed and closed her eyes forever. Frank held her hand as she slowly rose out of the straightjacket that held her and back into the spirit realm.

Ethan looked behind him. A vortex was opening and as the light got brighter two silhouettes could be seen coming through. He knew who they were and, as Kathleen joined him, she saw them too and smiled. Then she glanced at him.

"Everything will be alright now?" she said, half a statement and half a question. He nodded.

"Yes, Kathleen, everything will be fine now." He paused as her parents arrived then added, "Go and find peace, you deserve it."

She nodded and, without another word, went to her parents as they turned to make the journey back into the light, leaving Haniel and Ethan at the nursing home. Ethan turned around to look at Frank, who sat holding Kathleen's lifeless hand; he was still crying yet there was also a sense of returning lightness around him as if a great weight were being lifted from him.

"He will be okay, won't he?" Ethan asked. Haniel nodded, a smile on her beautiful face.

"Oh, yes, his prayers have been answered and once the grief has subsided he will enjoy life again for some years to come. Then when the time is right he will join Kathleen once more. Never fear, the Creator never means humans to suffer. Most of their pain is self-inflicted, but there is always another way and help available if asked for."

Ethan considered her words and had to agree again, which was getting a bit predictable, but still he knew from his own Earthly existence that he had worried about things he could do nothing about, giving himself a lot of extra stress and anxiety. He wasn't alone in that.

"I suppose you're right," he said, grudgingly.

Haniel laughed. "Of course I'm right. I'm an angel."

Ethan's mouth twitched at that, and he tried to stop a smile as he didn't want to encourage her; a comical, wisecracking angel would be hard to take. Haniel knew exactly what he was thinking. So many people believed angels were rather grand, solemn and humourless beings, yet the truth was so different. How could beings of light and love be anything but full of fun and joy? It just wasn't possible. Haniel sent blessings to Frank and then it was time for them also to leave.

"Take my hand," she said, and once he had they rose up together into the darkened sky. To Ethan, it took only a moment for them to return to the round building yet it had seemed to take him a lot longer to get to Earth. Haniel smiled. "Practice," she said.

CHAPTER 7

The Fear of Living

They retook their seats in the sunken garden and Ethan waited for the lecture he believed was coming, but he was wrong again.

"I think you have already learned all I could tell you, don't you?" She tilted her head as she looked at him so he smiled and nodded.

"Yes, I learned a lot, but then you knew I would."

"We should learn from every experience we have, but sadly that is not always the case, is it?" Ethan knew that all too well, as every human does.

"No, sometimes it takes more than one attempt to learn what we need to. Still, I learned a lot from Kathleen and I hope I helped her too."

"You did and she is at peace now." He was glad about that. Haniel looked at him again and smiled before she said, "So, you have chosen one person, only two more to go." He made a face and she laughed. "It isn't quite as easy as you imagined it would be?" she wondered, already knowing the answer.

"You know it isn't," he replied.

"But nothing is gained without a little effort, is it?"

He didn't answer that, as he had a nasty feeling that he was about to find out whom the second recipient would be and that they were going to be even more of a challenge than Kathleen. Haniel knew that he was right; there was someone she had in mind who could do with his help, yet his reasons for needing it were very different.

Kathleen had had a great fear of dying, which held her in her physical form, but Ben Harris wasn't scared to die. In fact, at times over the past four years, he would have embraced it, even longed for it, afraid to live, at least to the full. His soul was in torment and the anguish he was suffering was registered by his guide and guardian angel; but, until he asked for help, they could not intervene. For the last three months he had greatly suffered in silence, struggling on, until he finally broke down and got on his knees to ask for help. There was a small collective cheer in Heaven when he did so and now he could receive the help he needed. If Ben was quite what Ethan was expecting, Haniel wasn't sure, but he was what he was going to get if he agreed to carry on.

Ethan waited more than a little apprehensively and Haniel's smile made him even more uneasy as he shifted on the bench and looked down at his feet, wishing she'd get on with it and give him the bad news, as he was sure there was some coming.

"Well, Ethan," she began, "there is someone I have in mind who has asked for help."

"Oh yes?" he asked.

"Yes, he is in a lot of emotional pain and isn't one to ask for help easily, so it's taken him a while to pray."

Ethan nodded as he could relate to that. Once he had been too stubborn to ask another for help and this had cost him his life. It was never easy to realise that you need a hand, and pride can often get in the way, but eventually either you get help or go under. He had done the latter but it seemed that this man Haniel was talking about was a little brighter.

"What's the problem?" he asked, knowing that's what she wanted him to say.

She smiled and said, "Love."

His eyebrows shot up under his long, floppy fringe of dark brown hair. "Love?"

She nodded. "Yes, that's what I said."

"Isn't love a good thing?" he frowned.

"Of course it is," she said quickly. "Although it can cause a lot of problems as well," she added.

"Ain't that the truth," Ethan muttered. So many lives lost and even wars fought over the pursuit of love; just look at the trouble Helen of Troy caused. "So how is love the problem in this case then?"

She looked sad. "It's complicated," she said.

"Isn't it always?" Ethan grinned.

"Yes, it seems to be. But I'm an angel and we're not quite like you beings who have incarnated - we've never fallen in love with a single individual or hated another or felt jealousy, guilt, fear…"

"Enough, enough," Ethan cried and she giggled. "I get the point," he added. "You must despair at us mere mortals who suffer all these afflictions."

"Yes, sometimes we do, but these are all gifts from the Creator, so who are we to judge whether they are in your best interests or not?"

Ethan knew what she meant as he sometimes wondered if it had been a good idea to give humans their own free will; was it a gift or a curse? It could be both. It gave one the choice to screw up their life, to throw the proverbial spanner in the works and reap the consequences, although the alternative wasn't very inspiring or appealing either. On balance, he believed that having free will was much better than not having it, as long as you used it with a little thoughtfulness. Unfortunately, most humans didn't, which is why there is so much pain and heartache in the world.

"Okay. So love is this guy's problem. How?" he asked. "And don't say it's complicated as I already got that."

She grinned; he was catching on. "I wasn't going to," she said seriously, "but it is easier if I show you rather than tell you."

He tilted his head and looked at her. "Show me."

Seconds later they were both back looking down once more at the spinning Earth in the centre of the circular room. As Ethan watched, the picture was changing. Firstly, all he saw was clouds then gradually they parted and he found himself looking down at a house in a suburban street. He felt like he was watching a television, as it zoomed inside the house and onto a man sitting in a chair with his head in his hands. For some reason, Ethan was surprised by the person sitting in front of him although he wasn't quite sure why. The man was older than he thought he'd be, as he supposed that problems with love affected the young; clearly this wasn't really true at all. He began to study Ben Harris, a tall, athletic man with fine, light brown hair with just a touch of grey at the temples. His face was a strange one with high cheekbones and well-defined features, but it was the intensely blue eyes with their deep sadness that was his most striking feature. They say that the eyes are the windows to the soul and one look into his showed the depth of pain he was enduring. Ethan turned to Haniel, whose gentle, compassionate face looked sadly back at him.

"So, what happened to make him like this?" he asked.

In an instant, images appeared in his head just as with Kathleen and he understood them perfectly. He saw a younger version of the man before them, laughing and happy with a very pretty girl on his arm. Her name was Karen and they had met at college and married soon after. It had been a happy time and, for six years, they had lived in joy until they decided to start a family; but nothing happened, so they went to find out why and it was then that they discovered Karen had cancer. It had been a great shock but the doctors told them they had caught it early and, with treatment, she would recover. But they were wrong. Over the next two years, Karen's health faltered and slowly she deteriorated. Nothing had helped and in the end she was in so much pain that she begged them to let her die. It was up to Ben to do what she wanted and he stopped them giving her more useless treatments, so that she could die in peace and with dignity. It had been the hardest thing he had ever done, as he loved her so much, but in his heart he knew that it was the greatest show of his love for her that he could give. To love someone enough to let them go, to let them be free, was pure love.

So he nursed her those final few weeks and believed he'd never love again. At just twenty-seven years old, Karen died and Ben was bereft.

At first, he just couldn't believe she was gone; he continued to talk to her as if she were still there. His friends and family tried to get him out of the house but he dug his heels in and refused all their offers of help and support, until finally they just stopped trying; it was then that he began to come to terms with her death. Slowly, he looked outside of his house again and took a very small interest in the world.

He had a supportive boss who made it possible for him to work from home at first but then it became time to re-join his colleagues. Although it was hard at first, he knew that it was for the best and he was right. He needed other people around to stimulate his intellect and bring him back to life and he enjoyed their company, gradually embarking on a limited social life, mainly with friends, a drink after work, even a holiday in Jordan.

There was order, stability and a level of contentment in his life until Debbie joined the company... From the moment Ben set eyes on her, something unfroze inside him and he felt hot and tongue-tied whenever she came close. She unsettled him and he didn't like it, at first blaming her for the way she made him feel though he couldn't keep it up for long. Try as he might, he just could not stop thinking of her and the way she flicked back her long, blonde hair when she was nervous. There was a shyness hidden in her eyes and the soft tones of her voice were poetry to him, but she was a bit of a contradiction: on the surface she appeared self-confident, even cool and calculating, but if you studied her as Ben did you'd notice the lip she nibbled when she waited for your verdict on her work. Just like the hair-flick, it was an outward sign that she wasn't as sure of herself as she appeared. It was an act, but one she'd obviously practised as she did it so well. Ben found himself waiting for her arrival every day and, when she came, the sun also came out in his grey and mundane life; if for some reason she didn't go to work, he was miserable all day long.

He didn't want to face it but he was falling in love with her and he confided this in a moment of weakness to his sister, George (short for Georgina). She was delighted - until he had to admit that up until then he'd only spoken to her about work. George had given him a talking to and it had done the trick, he'd plucked up the courage to ask Debbie if she'd like to go to the pub for a drink after work. To his great surprise she'd said "Yes" and then he had been terrified, as his dating experience was very limited and it had been well over ten years since his last foray into the singles scene. But it had gone well and their relationship slowly developed.

However, Ben still had a problem, as he couldn't get Karen out of his head. He felt guilty for having feelings for another woman and he tried to explain it to George, but she just told him not to be so stupid and screw up this second chance of happiness, which didn't help him at all. On one level, he understood that Karen was gone and would have encouraged him to embrace love and take his chances but it still didn't feel right. He thought that, over time, these feelings would go away and he'd be comfortable with this new love but it hadn't happened like that at all and in fact, it had got worse. He loved Debbie and was sure she loved him. That was not the question - it was the feeling that it was wrong, like he was committing adultery, which kept him from being truly happy. He still felt he was married to Karen and that hadn't changed; what he longed for was a chance to talk to Karen and get her blessing. If he could do that then maybe he could finally work out what to do next.

Over the past three weeks, the urgency for a decision had increased as Debbie became impatient for him to commit to their relationship. He had resisted asking her to move in with him but time was not on his side and he knew that very soon he would receive an ultimatum: either he committed to her or she would walk away and he didn't know if he could handle that. Around and around his thoughts kept going, giving him no sleep and plenty of anxiety. He wasn't getting anywhere and it was driving him mad until finally, when all else had failed, he got down on his knees and for the first time in many years asked for some help. Only now could he receive it and the advice from his own guides - and from one special envoy from Heaven. If he accepted it, Ben could visit beyond the veil, as he seemed to be the lucky winner of a day trip to Heaven. Ethan finished watching the screen and looked up at Haniel.

"I see what you mean. Love isn't really his problem. I'd say it was guilt."

"Yes, you are right," Haniel agreed, "although loving someone too much to truly let them go is part of his problem."

"Okay, yes," he conceded grudgingly, then remembered something else: "And if you hold onto the memory of a person like Ben is doing, you can hinder their ability to move on in the spirit world." Haniel grinned; that was exactly what she'd hoped he would work out for himself and he hadn't disappointed her.

"That's right. Karen's time on Earth was over. She needed to move on and one of Ben's life lessons was to lose her. Now, you know that the Creator never gives you more trouble than you can cope with, don't you?"

"Yes, but a lot of people don't know that." Haniel pursed her lips and nodded but she found that hard to understand. Still, as she'd never lived on Earth, she had to accept what he said as the truth.

"That is unfortunate," she said before adding, "but nevertheless, before they had incarnated, they had agreed to fall in love and marry, with the knowledge that Karen would leave after a few years."

"So, if they agreed this before incarnating," Ethan frowned, "why doesn't he let her go now?"

"He's forgotten. And he hasn't used his gifts to find the answers to all those questions he still has."

"His gifts?" Ethan queried. "What gifts?"

Haniel sighed. Sometimes it was so very hard to watch talented people ignore the great gifts that God had given them to use on their life's journey, solely because they either didn't value them or didn't realise they existed. Everyone has gifts but if they are not used then they are wasted, along with many opportunities to further spiritual growth.

"He would be able to answer all his questions if he had continued his meditation practice. Karen was instrumental in getting him interested in his spiritual side and they meditated together. He has a lot of psychic abilities too and was making such good progress. But after she died he gave it all up."

"Ah, yes, now I understand. But if he's lost his faith and turned his back on his gifts and beliefs, how can I help him?"

"By taking him up to the Hall of Records, so he can understand that Karen died at the right time for her and for him, that this was arranged by both their souls before they came back to Earth. He has to see that what has happened did so for a reason. Karen has other work to do now, but he is preventing her from doing this by holding her close to him, as he has been doing. Also, he has nothing to be guilty about as he cared for her, loved her and that is all she ever needed. Now, he must see that it is imperative he moves on in his life's journey - there is so much left for him to discover for his own growth before he returns home."

She was passionate in her discourse and Ethan couldn't hide a small smile. She, he believed, had a soft spot for this man and he wasn't sure if that was allowed. Haniel stopped talking and immediately picked up his thoughts. "Alright, clever clogs, you may be right and, no, I don't suppose we should have favourites but we are only angels." She shrugged dramatically and he burst out laughing.

"Only angels?" he spluttered in high amusement.

She grinned, enjoying her conversations with him a lot. She had often heard people use the phrase 'only human' and wished she could shake them and say, "You are so much more." Of course, she never had, but now it was her turn; being an angel meant immortality, so over time she had witnessed everything that humankind could experience and do to one another. At times, their behaviour had sickened her but at others it was heroic and inspirational; she hoped that Ben would become all he could be, though she had to admit he needed a little help. That's where Ethan came in so she looked him in the eye and said, "Well, are you going to help him or not?"

Ethan rolled his eyes. "Do I have a choice?"

She smiled and said, innocently, "Of course you do."

He wasn't so sure but nodded anyway. "Then I'll help him."

Her smile grew larger as she replied, "So, what are you waiting for?"

CHAPTER 8

Dream Visitors

Now that he'd accepted the challenge, Ethan was faced with the practicality of how to do it. It was time for a little help so he turned to Haniel.

"Alright," she offered, "I suggest you approach him in his sleep as dreams are often the way guides and angels get messages through to humans. So when he's asleep, you will find him more receptive and it will be much more likely that he will follow you to the Hall of Records." Ethan could see the logic in that.

"Yes, okay, and once we get to the Hall of Records, what then?"

"Well, that is up to him."

"Please don't go all cryptic on me again," he groaned through gritted teeth. She giggled at his pained expression.

"I can't do everything for you," she said, much to his annoyance.

"I'm not asking you to," he retorted. "All I want is a little guidance now and again." She sniffed.

"You'll be the one giving guidance soon and you can't keep running to us for help. So, get used to it."

He was surprised by the forceful tone in her voice; he'd never heard an angel with raised voice before. Was he so aggravating that he could make even an angel lose her patience? He looked up at her and was relieved to see that she was smiling.

"That got your attention, didn't it?" she said and he nodded, as it had indeed. "Good, so let me say one more thing, which is relevant for Ben and to the soul you will soon be guiding. Things happen." He waited for more but, after a while, realised that was all he was getting.

"Things happen?" he repeated and she nodded.

"That's right," she said, as if that explained everything. He decided he wouldn't ask what the heck that meant but, instead, he'd think quietly about it.

"Things happen," he muttered and then it came to him in a flash, in one of what he had always called his 'eureka moments'. "So, when things happen, we have to adapt, see the bigger picture and go with the flow."

"By Jove, I think you've got it," she said in a clipped British accent.

And she had to admit he really had at last got the message that life was about the choices we make. One choice will lead us in one direction but a different choice could lead somewhere totally different; so, things happen, life changes, outcomes are altered and the path leads somewhere unexpected. All he could do was lead Ben to the Hall of Records and see what happened. That was, in essence, the job of all guides, to give options and support, then wait to see what becomes of it as it wasn't his job to tell anyone what they should or should not do; that wasn't guidance, that was control. It wasn't easy, sitting back and letting another make their own decisions and their own mistakes but it had to be done. It was a bit like parenting: there always comes a time when you have to let go and hope that you have brought the children up so they can take responsibility for their own lives and choose wisely. Too much help isn't the answer but neither is too little guidance, so it's a balancing act and never easy to achieve. Haniel nodded, reading his thoughts.

"No, it isn't easy but it is essential for a guide to know the boundaries and not cross them." She paused and then added, "So, let us wait for our opportunity to guide this troubled soul."

Ben lay in bed, staring at the ceiling and trying to stop his mind from going around in endless and pointless circles as he still didn't know how to resolve his problem. He loved Debbie but it wasn't like his love for Karen - so was he really then in love? Could he trust these feelings? Would Karen have liked her? Was this right? Why did he feel so guilty? He turned on his side and sighed heavily as it was no good, he couldn't decide what to do and nothing he'd tried had, so far, helped him either.

"I need divine help," he thought, as he closed his eyes.

Haniel looked at Ethan and they both moved closer to his bed and waited as finally Ben's breathing became deeper and more rhythmic as he drifted into sleep. His eyes flickered as he entered a REM cycle. This was what Ethan had been waiting for and he focused on tuning into Ben's dreams as Haniel had instructed him. Within a few seconds, he reached Ben and found himself in a stairway, a very functional stairway like one would find in any office block anywhere in the world. He watched as Ben ran up and down the stairs, reminding him of a hamster on a wheel going nowhere fast.

"This won't do," he said and stepped out in front of Ben, bringing him to a screeching halt. Ben stood before him, his eyes wide open in surprise, dumbstruck by Ethan's sudden appearance. Ethan just smiled.

"Hello, I'm here to help you." Ben shut his open mouth and frowned at the smaller, slimmer figure in front of him.

"Help me?" he queried, unsure if he'd heard him correctly.

"Yes, that's right," Ethan nodded, then tilted his head slightly to one side before adding, "You did ask for help, didn't you?" Ben nodded. "Well, here I am," Ethan said as he held out his arms.

The frown on Ben's face deepened as this almost fragile-looking man wasn't the kind of help he was hoping for; after all, what could he do to resolve his dilemma? Ethan knew what he was thinking and smiled.

"I know," he said, "you're thinking 'Who the hell is this guy who says he can help me'? Am I right?" Ben nodded again. "Well, believe it or not, I was sent here because you asked for help. Oh and by the way, you should have done that a lot sooner and saved yourself some pain." Ethan enjoyed the look of surprise and confusion on Ben's face. "Still, eventually you got the message so better late than never, I always say. So, here I am ready, willing and able to give you a hand if you still want it." He paused, then added. "It's your decision." It was the deep hopelessness he felt inside that convinced Ben that any help, even from this man, was better than none.

"I accept your offer," he said weakly. "What can you do?" Ethan grinned.

"I can take you to a very special place called the Hall of Records."

Ben had never heard of such a place. "The Hall of Records?"

"Yep, that's right. It's where all the books ever written are kept. But it's more than just a library, it's where Akashic records of every life ever lived are stored." Ben had heard of Akashic records but it was hard to believe what he was being told.

"Every life?" he queried. Ethan nodded.

"Every lifetime of every soul that has ever incarnated. It is truly an amazing place."

"You've been there?"

"Oh yes, many times, and so have you, only you don't remember it."

Ben pointed to his chest and said, "I've been there?"

"Yep, lots of times. In fact, before you incarnated, you visit the Hall of Records with your guide to review your past lives and decide on what you wanted to learn and achieve in this one."

"Past lives? So, we live more than once then?" Ben asked softly, as if he were addressing himself more than Ethan.

It was then that Ethan began to understand the level on the spiritual path than Ben had reached before Karen's death and he'd given up. He was still very much a beginner, just exploring the concepts and what lay beyond the physical world. Somehow, he'd expected him to be further along the path than that. His job, he felt, had just got a lot tougher.

"Yes, you've lived many lives and if you come with me you can find out all about them for yourself."

"And that will help me?"

"Yes, it will," Ethan nodded.

"How?"

Ethan grinned. He'd been hoping he wouldn't ask but, since he had, all he could do was to tell him the truth. "I don't know," he said. Ben looked shocked and, for a few seconds, he was speechless.

"You don't know? What are you saying? You're not making any sense at all."

Ethan nodded his agreement.

"You're right. It may not make sense in the logical, analytical world in which you live but, in the spirit world, that doesn't matter. You have to believe that I was sent here to help you and told to take you to the Hall of Records and that was all I was told to do. Now, I knew that you wouldn't be allowed to go there unless it was to help you make your mind up after you get more information. This is a once in a lifetime, limited offer - you either accept it now, this instant, or not at all. That's up to you but this offer won't be repeated."

"I have to make up my mind now?" Ben asked.

"Yes, now. So what's it to be, are you going to take a leap of faith or stay put, confused and unhappy?" Ben wasn't sure, but if this man was the only help he was going to get, he'd better accept it.

"Well, as you put it like that, I guess I'm going to the Hall of Records," he said.

"A wise choice," Ethan replied and, with a snap of his fingers, they found themselves standing in front of a massive, classical Greco-Roman building with towering marble columns and a breath-taking dome that seemed to reach up forever. In front of them were a series of gleaming white steps that went up to a pair of massive, golden doors glowing in the sunlight. Ethan smiled and looked over at his companion, who stared wide-eyed at the awesome sight before them.

'And that's just the outside,' Ethan thought, as he knew that the interior was even more magnificent. "Beautiful, isn't it?" he said and Ben nodded.

"Yes, it is and it's so…" He ran out of words to describe it, as there weren't any that could really do it justice. Ethan grinned.

"Yep, it is everything you could say and then some but wait 'til you see the inside."

Ben shook his head. "I don't think I can be more impressed," he said, dragging his eyes away from the incredible structure to look at his guide. Ethan raised an eyebrow.

"Oh, I think you can," he said, starting up the steps. "Come on, let's see if I'm right."

Ben hesitated just for a moment before he too set off up the marble steps, counting as he went; by the time he'd got to the top, he had counted fifty steps and was a little breathless. Ethan wasn't but then he understood that, in Heaven, you could choose to work hard as if you were in a physical body or not and, as he always hated exercise on Earth, he didn't intend to start doing any now. He was quite amused at the sight of Ben panting up the stairs when he could have floated above them as he had done, but then there is always someone who wants to do things the hard way. They stood together, looking up at the golden doors that towered over them to a height of more than thirty feet.

"Wow, these doors are so beautiful," Ben said, as he ran his fingers over the intricate patterns moulded into each panel. Every one was different but they all contained patterns rather than figures, some very geometric while others were abstract, although they were all very detailed and perfectly made. Ben felt he should recognise these patterns; it was as if they were familiar to him but, as hard as he tried, he just couldn't remember where he might have seen something similar before. Ethan knew what he was thinking and understood why he felt as he did, for these patterns were ancient and came from very early Earth civilisations, such as the Maya, Inca and Atlantis, places where people had incarnated centuries before. There were memories of these times still locked into people's subconscious, which was why these panels often triggered thoughts from lives lived so long ago. But however beautiful the doors were, they were not the reason for their being here. It was time to move on and, as Ethan thought this, the great doors began to open and they stepped back standing side-by-side as, slowly and silently, the massive doors slid apart to reveal a space so vast as to be beyond imagination. They stepped inside a gigantic library with aisle after aisle of shelves as far as the eye could see into infinity.

"Oh, my God," Ben said, almost in a whisper.

"Um, I did say you'd be impressed," Ethan replied, somewhat smugly.

"It's more than impressive."

Ben was mesmerised by the vastness of it all; it was also a little frightening, a space that appeared to have no limits or boundaries, a maze of shelves and aisles in which you could quite literally get lost. He wasn't at all sure he wanted to go any further in, just in case he couldn't get back out again, but Ethan wasn't going to allow him to stop there and he nudged him into forward motion.

"Come on, it's not going to swallow you or anything and re-member, you're here for a reason. So let's get on with it." Ben frowned and turned to his guide.

"I thought you didn't know why I'm here," he said, accusingly.

Ethan raised an eyebrow at his tone. "I don't know exactly," he said, evasively.

"But you do know more than you're telling me and I'm not go-ing a single step further until you tell me everything you know." He stopped in the middle of the central aisle and glared at Ethan, a look of obstinacy on his strong face.

"I sure know how to pick them,' he muttered. Then, knowing he'd not move Ben until he told him what he knew, he decided to spill the beans although, quite frankly, he had very few to spill.

"Okay, so you're here to read your own Akashic record and that's all I know, cross my heart," he said with his arms raised up in surrender.

Ben frowned. "And that is going to help me with my decision?"

"I don't know," Ethan shrugged. "It's not my life's record or my decision. I'm only the messenger. What you do with the message is up to you."

For a few moments, they stood a few feet apart, staring at each other until Ben broke the standoff and the defiance left his body. He turned around to look at the shelves all around him.

"So, somewhere in here is a book with my name on it?" he asked. Ethan smiled as it wasn't quite the way things worked, but close.

"Yes, well, something like that," he replied.

"So, how on Earth do we find it?"

Ethan chuckled at the vexed expression on Ben's face. "Well, for starters, we are not on Earth but that's not the point, I know," he said, quickly. "Don't look so worried, we don't have to look at every one to find yours - you will be guided to it."

"Guided?"

"Yes, all you have to do is focus on the record and let your feet do the rest."

"I do that by myself?"

"Yes, sure, well, I mean, I can't help you there, pal. After all, it's your record you want to find, not mine."

"And you can't find mine?" Ben asked.

"Nope, you're the only one who has the right to read it. There are occasionally exceptions to that rule but they don't apply here, so you've got to do it on your own."

Ben had many more questions he'd like to have asked but he didn't think it was probably the best time to ask them, as his guide appeared to be getting a bit ratty with him, so he decided he'd give it a go.

"Alright then, do I close my eyes and focus or what?"

Ethan had to smile at the image his words had conjured up as he could just see him bumping into shelves, knocking things flying and then spending the next hundred years putting everything back. He shook his head.

"Good God, no. You'll end up neck-deep in books if you do that. Just stand there and clear your mind of everything except your intention to find your Akashic record and then, if you're concentrated enough, you'll feel compelled to go in one direction. Don't analyse what you feel, just go with it. If you think too much, you'll never find it."

Ben frowned as it all sounded very cockeyed to him but, if Ethan said this is how he should do it, who was he to argue? "Right, got it," he said.

"Well, good," Ethan replied, somewhat uncertainly. "I'll be by your side all the time. Okay?"

"Okay."

Ben stood still and began to focus as somewhere in this vast building was the book he needed. At first, it was hard to think only of that and exclude all the other thoughts that cluttered his mind but, eventually, he could see it and knew he had to turn around and take the next aisle on the right. How he knew this he didn't stop to analyse, he just turned and headed in that direction.

★

CHAPTER 9

The Hall of Records

Ben set off at quite a pace down the central aisle then turned right and carried on walking with Ethan in his wake. He came to a crossroads and stopped, so suddenly that Ethan had to take evasive action to avoid colliding with him; he looked at Ben's face and it was a picture of concentration, his eyes closed, and a slight frown across his forehead, his lips pursed. After a few moments, his expression changed and he was off again, turning left and then right. As they went deeper into the library, they passed others who were also doing research but Ben seemed totally oblivious to any of them as he focused on his mission until finally he stopped, turned and reached up onto a shelf, removing with both hands a large leather-bound volume. He sighed and held it to his chest, a look of triumph and relief on his face.

"This is it," he said. Ethan nodded and smiled, impressed by his level of concentration, something he himself had always had problems with.

"Okay, let's take it to the lectern and you can look at it." It was only then that Ben realised they were not alone; at the end of each row of shelves was a lectern where the books could be placed and read easily, and at a lot of these were people already reading.

"Who are all these people?" he asked.

"Some are just like you and others need to review their past lives to start planning their future ones." He turned and pointed across to the right, where two figures stood. "Like those two over there. You see, the woman reading the record is preparing to incarnate and the male figure behind her is her gatekeeper."

Ben frowned. "Gatekeeper? Who is he and what does he do?"

Ethan sighed inwardly as he shouldn't have used this title but, as he had, he'd have to explain what he meant.

"The gatekeeper is your life guide and they work with you before you incarnate, as that one is doing, helping you plan who will be your parents, where you'll live and your life's lessons and challenges. Then he or she will stay with you when you return to Earth and look after you."

"Like a bodyguard?" Ben asked. Ethan shook his head.

"Not quite. They are more a protector of your soul. They can't stop you from hurting yourself or making bad decisions, nor can they save you from danger, but they can help you if you ask."

"And everyone has one of these?" Ben asked.

"Of course, but you also have other guides who may be there for a long time or just to help over a difficult period, a bit like specialists. You know, like doctors - if you have an illness, often a doctor with knowledge of this disease will come to you. They wait for you to ask for help or guidance and then give it to you." Ethan paused, before, "It's a great pity more people don't know about them. If they did, they could get so much help and save themselves a lot of unnecessary suffering."

Ben grimaced at that less-than-subtle dig at his own refusal to ask for help earlier, but he still didn't understand. "These protectors?"

"Gatekeepers," Ethan corrected.

"Are they the guardian angels people talk about?"

Ethan sighed and wondered why human beings gave angels all the credit when it was guides who did all the hard work...

"No, they are not angels. Angels can't guide you. They've never incarnated as they are from a totally separate realm, or dimension.

THE HALL OF RECORDS

Believe me, you don't want to get too mixed up with them, they're a whole different kettle of fish entirely." Behind him, Ethan thought he heard someone giggle but, when he looked, there was no-one there.

"So, the gatekeepers are humans who are now helping people on Earth?"

"That's it in a nutshell."

"So, I have one?" Ben queried.

"Sure," Ethan answered.

"Then where are they when I need them?"

"Oh," Ethan grinned, "she's right behind you."

Ben didn't move for what seemed like twenty seconds, then he swung around and, sure enough, there she was in all her glory. His mouth dropped as he took her in. She stood all of five foot tall, a very shapely, curvaceous yet perfect figure dressed in a classic white dress straight out of the pages of Homer's Odyssey. Her long, blonde hair tumbled down in waves and ringlets onto her bare shoulders and her impish face seemed almost too small and delicate to house such large, blue eyes. She giggled as both of them stared in more than casual curiosity, as she was like something out of a Greek myth, maybe a goddess. Finally, Ben managed to speak again.

"Are you my gatekeeper?" he asked.

"Yes, I am," she nodded.

"But you're…" He didn't know what he'd been expecting but she wasn't it; she knew what he was thinking and was disappointed. He'd thought he'd get some warrior, a monk or, Heaven forbid, a Red Indian.

"Well, if that's what you want," she said, "I can give it to you." Suddenly, the goddess disappeared and was replaced by a knight in armour. "I can be like this if you prefer," a deep voice said from below all the tin. Then he disappeared to be replaced by a monk in a brown habit. "Or this." Then he, too, disappeared and a Native American girl in buckskin stood before them. "Or this? I've lived four hundred and thirty-three lives, so take your pick, whichever one makes you most comfortable, I'll be."

Ben frowned as maybe he'd expected a fighting man to protect him but, if he could choose, he'd forego that and pick the goddess instead; before he had time to say this, the goddess was back with a huge smile on her face.

"I'm glad you chose this image as I had one of my best lives as Kalistra," she said.

"Kalistra, that's a beautiful name," Ben replied.

"Thank you, and I'm so glad you have finally come to your senses and asked for help."

Ethan grimaced but then a small smile touched his lips as he'd never had a guide that looked like Kalistra; some people had all the luck. He shook his head to clear it of such thoughts and returned to why they were here in the first place.

"Yes, well, Ben," he said seriously, "let's get on, shall we? Now your guide is here, take the book and look at it together."

"Together?" Is that alright? I thought you said I was the only one to read it."

"Did I?" Ethan replied.

"Yes, you did," Ben retorted.

"Oh, sorry. Well, as Kalistra helped you plan this life, she already knows what's in it. Isn't that right?" He looked at the goddess, who smiled and nodded.

"Yes but I can only help you if you'll let me," she said to Ben, who nodded humbly and followed her to a lectern where he laid down the book of lives. Ethan watched them from a distance, as Ben opened the book and took a deep breath before beginning to read.

Ethan wandered a little distance away. He wasn't part of this and felt left out. But maybe, after this, he would have fulfilled his duties and then he'd have only one person left to help. 'What a relief,' he thought.

"Be careful what you wish for," a light, feminine voice said in his ear.

"Haniel?" He couldn't see her at first but, slowly, she became visible by his side.

"How is it going?" she asked, although she already knew.

He wasn't falling for that. He rolled his eyes and didn't reply as they stood together in silence, watching Ben and Kalistra studying the book. Ethan was curious about what was in it but he knew that wasn't for him to see; instead, he'd have to be patient and wait for them to finish.

Ben read the current page slowly, trying to take it all in. Firstly it gave the name he had chosen for this lifetime, which was David. He frowned and looked at Kalistra.

"David?" he queried.

"Yes, that was the name you chose, as it had the right vibrational quality for your lifetime. But your parents were determined to have Ben, even though they felt it wasn't right for you."

"So, would my life be different if my name were David instead of Ben?"

She nodded. "In some respects it would be, as names are very important. They are part of you in the lifetime that you carry them in. That's why some people look like a Julia or a Gary - it suits them and is an enhancement to their growth. But when the name you are given isn't right for you, it can hold you back. Haven't you ever thought about changing your name?" He nodded.

"Yes, I have, I've never liked the name Ben, it's never felt, I don't know, me. But I couldn't decide what I wanted to be called either." She grinned.

"David means 'beloved' and I think you'd be a lot happier if you changed Ben for that."

"But everyone will think I've gone crazy," he said.

"Not if you say it's your middle name and you prefer it. It may take a few weeks for people to get used to it but they will, and you'll find life flowing a lot easier once you do."

He wasn't so sure but he'd think about it. They returned to the book and he saw that he'd lived lives with both his parents before;

one was with the soul of his mother who had created a large karmic debt, which she owed him. In this lifetime, she tended to smother him with love, to be over-protective when he was a child and an interfering mother as a teenager and adult, as she was trying to pay off the debt. Instead, she was creating new problems. He sighed.

"What can I do about that?" he asked.

"Tell her she is forgiven," Kalistra smiled. "Even if consciously she doesn't understand, her subconscious will and this over-protective behaviour will slowly disappear. You will have to be patient with her and keep telling her you forgive her, then this will happen if you mean it." He smiled.

"I do forgive her. I understand why she feels guilty but I don't want her to."

"Then it will work when you tell her she is forgiven and loved."

"I will," he nodded, and they again returned to the book. He read on and found another surprise. "I'm in the wrong job?" he exclaimed and Kalistra smiled. She could have told him that if he'd only asked; he looked at her and saw her smile. "You knew?"

"Of course, but I can't interfere, only guide. If you'd asked for guidance, I'd have given it but you never did until now."

He thought about her words and realised that she was right; he had a major problem about asking for help. Somehow he thought it weak but perhaps he'd got that wrong too. He was certainly coming face-to-face with himself and it wasn't a very comfortable experience. He read the passage again and began to understand where and how he'd strayed off his life path. At college, he had always been concerned with the disadvantaged and the poor, both at home and abroad. He campaigned, went on marches and petitioned, but nothing seemed to change, so gradually he stopped going and, as his final exams got closer, he decided he needed to put all his energies into passing them. Then, he had told himself, he'd get back to helping others. But, if he were truthful, he didn't really mean it and in his heart he knew he was giving up; but he couldn't admit that, even to himself. So the first opportunities to work for others slipped past. He passed his Finals and, to pay off the debts he'd run up at college, took a job he was offered at a computer company. It was very good money and, again, he lied to himself, denying his true calling, saying he'd work there just long enough to get back in the black and then he'd help others. Then the second opportunity to start on his life's work passed him by. For several years he worked on computers, getting promotions along with salary increases to match; he married Karen, got a mortgage and told himself he had responsibilities now, so he couldn't possibly take the large cut in wages that would be required if he worked for a charity. He was very convincing and, on the surface, he believed it. But deep down he was unhappy in denying who he truly was. It was like he had an itch that he couldn't scratch and it niggled at the deep recesses of his mind; he knew it would continue to do so unless he did something about it.

"Well?" he asked Kalistra.

She raised her delicate, blonde eyebrows and shrugged. "It's up to you," she said.

"That's not very helpful," he replied and she giggled.

"No, maybe not, but I can only help you discover your talents, see your options and choices, then only you can act on them."

"Okay, I understand that. So, what are my options?"

She looked at him to see if he was serious and found, a little to her surprise, that he was.

"Well," she said, "let's start with your talents. You're logical but not in a pedantic way."

He frowned at that. "Is that good or bad?"

"Oh, it's good," she assured him before continuing. "You are a good organiser and have great people-management skills - you get the best out of people without bullying or humiliating them." He agreed with that although, until she said it, he'd never thought of it as a talent.

"You are empathic but can still remain detached and unemotional. You also have a social conscience and believe in justice. You are responsible, trustworthy and, once you commit to doing something, you don't give up so you're not a quitter and that is really important for this life's lessons you have chosen to fulfil. You will need to persevere, but you can succeed and in doing so really make a difference for a lot of people."

"I can make a difference?" he asked, unsure she was talking about him or maybe she'd mixed him up with someone else.

"Yes you, little old you." She sighed dramatically and shook her head. "You know, I get a little tired of hearing you putting yourself down, the constant 'I'm not good enough'. Bullshit," she said loudly and he started in surprise. It just wasn't a word he'd ever imagined a sweet, delicate creature like her would even know, let alone use. She was pleased her use of the word had made him take some notice, so she continued. "You are good enough to do whatever you truly, madly and deeply want to do. You don't need anyone's approval or blessing, except your own. To be really happy and fulfilled, you need to decide what you are going to do with the rest of your life and now is as good a time as any. In fact, it's the perfect time."

"Why's that?"

"Because there is no-one else in the equation. No more excuses, so you can follow your heart or live a lie. The choice is all yours."

CHAPTER 10

Changes of Heart and Mind

The words 'the choice is all yours' really hit a sore spot in Ben and he realised in that split second how often he'd considered everyone else and their feelings before he did anything - and how he didn't do what he really wanted to because it might upset someone else. He had given up his life's path to appease and accommodate others who so often, in the end, didn't appreciate or acknowledge his sacrifice.

'But to do only what you want to do maybe isn't that selfish,' he thought. Kalistra heard him and answered immediately.

"No, it's not selfish. In fact, you have been quite rude to the Creator by not following your calling or using, for the good of others, the talents He bestowed on you. It cannot be selfish to follow your life path, can it?" He didn't need to think about it and knew deep down she was right.

"No, I see that now," he acknowledged.

"So, what are you going to do about it?" she asked him.

"I'm going to follow my heart, not my head," he replied. "You're right, I have no responsibilities now, no reason not to do what's right for me. I mean, I've paid off my mortgage so my outgoings are now a lot smaller. I could take a cut in wages and still be okay."

The more he thought about it, the more excited he got as it was like something had been released inside of him. He felt lighter and more optimistic about the future than he had in years. He had recently become involved with a charity that helped communities in Third World countries to obtain clean water and taught them about hygiene and sanitation. What he liked about this charity was that it didn't do everything for those in need: it worked with local groups that do their share of the work, digging wells and learning how to maintain the pumps. It also worked with women, teaching them the importance of hygiene and sanitation to stop the killer illnesses of diarrhoea and dysentery that killed so many children every year; then those women taught other women and, like dropping a pebble into a still pool, the ripples spread outwards until it reached the neighbouring villages that wanted clean water, hygiene and sanitation too. He knew this was the kind of organisation for which he wanted to work, maybe do some hands-on work in the field too. Kalistra was delighted that he now had something on which to focus that would bring him the personal joy and fulfilment that, up to now, he'd denied himself.

There was just one more area of his life that he needed to look at and it was the most complex and difficult one, so she took an inward deep breath before broaching the subject.

"Now we come to your personal relationships," she said.

"That's a disaster area," he grimaced. She couldn't agree more but it had to be tackled and tackled now, so she wasn't going to let him wriggle out of discussing it.

"It hasn't always been so," she said softly. He sighed.

"No, once upon a time, it was the best area in my life."

She indicated that they should return to look in the book. "Maybe you'll find more answers in here."

He didn't look too enthusiastic about that but moved back to the lectern anyway. To his surprise, he found that Karen and he had agreed before incarnating to marry in this lifetime; but the real surprise was that her death from cancer had also been planned.

"But why?" he asked Kalistra.

"Because she had a lesson to learn from such a death and you had to learn how to let go of someone you love. Together, you could both fulfil a need and grow."

He didn't want to believe her and couldn't accept that he would have agreed to lose her so quickly. Why would he do such a thing? Kalistra knew that he would rail against this, as he still hadn't really come to terms with Karen's death, but the book didn't lie. They had made a contract and he wasn't holding up his end of the bargain. She had to make him see this.

"You do realise that by holding on to her memory as tightly as you do, you are also stopping her soul moving forward as well?" He frowned.

"How does that work?"

"Well, Karen had to learn a lesson, which if you read between the lines here was to die with grace and dignity, to accept it and not fight it." Ben's frown deepened.

"But aren't we supposed to fight death?"

"No. Death is not an enemy - it can be a friend. Death of the physical body is not death of the soul because the soul is immortal. Our lives on Earth are just excursions to a denser plane of existence where we can learn things we can't learn here in the spirit worlds."

"But why does it have to hurt so much?" he raged.

"Because the soul only learns from personal experiences." She paused to let him think before she continued. "Do you learn more from everything going smoothly and according to plan, or do you learn more from surmounting difficulties, perseverance and, yes, even painful experiences?" She looked at his troubled face and waited for his reply. Finally, he sagged and gave in.

"From the hard times," he said, reluctantly. He didn't want it to be so but it was and he couldn't make it any other way.

"Yes, I know it seems harsh but on Earth you have a saying, I think: 'Tough love'. Some lives on Earth are like that." He knew what she meant, even if she hadn't quite got it right.

"Then you're saying that Karen learned her lesson and her soul is now ready to move on and learn something else."

Kalistra nodded. "Yes, if you will let her."

"But I still miss her," he muttered. She did understand although he needed to stop holding on to the past and start living in the present. She glanced at the book once more to see if there was something she could use to convince him there was light at the end of the tunnel. She found it.

"Ben, look here."

She pointed further down the page and he moved closer to get a better look. There in black and white was another contract he had made with another soul, that they would marry and have two children; the frown reappeared on his face.

"I made this agreement?" he asked. She smiled and nodded.

"Yes, of course you did or it wouldn't be here. Although, if you don't move on with your life, you will block this other soul's entry into your life. Then you'll be responsible for holding up not just Karen's development but yours and this incoming soul's as well."

A shiver went through him at her words, as it was clear that wasn't a good thing to do at all and the consequences could be very challenging; but he still didn't feel ready to give up the love he felt for Karen, though he didn't want to hurt her either. He had come here to ask her permission to commit to Debbie and, instead, what he should be doing was asking her to forgive him for holding her back. She had moved into spirit at what was the right time for her, even if it hadn't seemed so for him, and there was nothing he could do about that but accept it. She wasn't coming back.

"Alright, I know I have to say goodbye and this time mean it for both our sakes, but it just won't be easy."

Kalistra understood. "It's never easy, but if we love someone we have to let them be free." He nodded and she patted his arm. "So, let's see what the future could hold for you if you really want it." There, on the page was the contract - only it wasn't Debbie's name on it but someone he'd never heard of.

"The name's wrong," he stated.

Kalistra's expression didn't change. "Is it?" she queried.

"Yes, it is. If I'm going to marry Deb…" Then it dawned on him. "I'm not going to marry Debbie, am I?"

Kalistra shrugged. "Don't ask me. It's entirely your decision whom you marry. I can't stop you."

"But she isn't the woman I made a contract with, is she? She's not the one."

Kalistra smiled but didn't reply, although she didn't really need to. He knew, deep down inside, that this was right. Kalistra then added another theory he hadn't thought of.

"Maybe it is Debbie, only her spirit name is different, like yours should have been David. Perhaps hers should have been this Gemma."

"Mmm, yes, that might be it," he said slowly, as only first names are written in the book.

"Anyway, when you change one area of your life, it has consequences on all the other areas."

"Yes, I understand that," he nodded. "So if I follow my true life path and change my career, the whole of my lifestyle will have to be different too. I won't have much spare cash anymore, though I'm not worried about that. I'll miss my work colleagues, as I don't have many friends outside work, although I'm bound to have new colleagues and friends. The real bonus will be a feeling that I'm doing something positive, both for the planet and my fellow man."

He knew he had to do it. Working with soulless machines just didn't satisfy him anymore, if it ever really had. No, if nothing else came out of this experience, he was convinced that he had to follow his calling and change his job; the rest, as they say, would take care of itself. He also knew Debbie well enough to suspect that she had no intention of having children or marrying a lowly charity worker; so, in a way, he had his answer. He read to the end of the page and was about to turn it when Kalistra stopped him.

"No, Ben, you have seen enough for now."

"But what happens next?" he wanted to know.

"That's for you to figure out," she smiled. "Don't you have enough to work on already?" she said, as she lifted his book off the lectern and handed it to him. "It's time for me to go now - I am always with you, even though you'll not see me quite as clearly as this again except in meditation or, maybe, the odd dream or two."

"Where are you going?" he asked, a bit of panic in his voice. She smiled.

"Don't worry, Ethan has more to show you." He didn't look any happier at that. "Trust me, you'll gain from it and, remember, you can't get rid of me. I'm your gatekeeper. I'm with you for life." He nodded.

"I'm glad about that. And I've decided to start meditating again."

"Then we will meet often," she said, smiling. "So, it is only a brief farewell until we meet again." And with that she vanished.

Ethan saw Kalistra disappear and he looked at Haniel.

"So, that's it, is it? Do I take him back now?" he asked hopefully, though he had a feeling that it wasn't to be. Again, he was right. Haniel still had work for him to do.

"No, I think Ben would benefit from a small tour here."

"A tour?"

"Yes, a small tour," she replied.

"And this tour... exactly where do you want me to take him?"

"Oh, well, just have a walk around and maybe visit the Hall of Justices gardens," she replied, rather vaguely.

He wasn't fooled by her act. She wanted him, for some reason she wasn't going to tell him, to take Ben into the gardens. Well, he'd do it as it was no hardship to walk in such beauty, but he also knew that something would happen while they were there. He sighed as he did feel a bit used. But then, when he did become a guide – if that ever happened – he might often feel like that or worse; he could be totally ignored. Haniel patted his arm and smiled.

"No-one could ignore you." He wasn't sure if that was meant as a compliment but decided to take it as one.

"Thank you," he replied sweetly and Haniel laughed before pushing him, ever so gently, towards his charge. Ben stood with a kind of glazed look in his eyes, which was probably appropriate, seeing that he'd discovered a life-changing experience. Ethan spoke to him and made him start in surprise.

"Hey, you okay?" Ethan asked. Ben recovered his composure and nodded.

"Yes, it's just... well... there was... you know..." he said and Ethan smiled.

"Yes, pal, I do know. It's all a bit confusing at first but let it sink in and, when you wake up, you'll know exactly what to do next."

Ben frowned. "Wake up? You mean this is just a dream, it's not real?" Ethan shook his head.

"Now, did I say that?" he replied. "What I'm saying is, this is real, what you read is real, but to absorb this information we needed you to relax and let go. You'd given up meditation, which is the other way to talk to any of us in spirit, by the way. So, with that option closed off, contact was made through your dreams. Luckily for you, I came along when I did - though I doubt it was down to luck." He paused then added, "Anyway, I've been given permission to take you on a little tour."

"A tour?" Ben asked, just as Ethan had done before him. Ethan grinned; he had an echo.

"Yep, a tour, only a little one but it'll be worth it. That is, unless you've got something better to do?" Ben shook his head.

"No, no, I'd love to see more if I'm allowed."

Ethan gestured they should go and, as they began to retrace their steps, he added, "Permission granted. You might say, omission denied."

Ben wasn't sure what he meant by that but he didn't care as he was going to get to see a bit more of Heaven and that was okay by him. They found the central aisle and headed for the door, passing on the way other people who were busy reading books. One man in particular caught Ben's attention as he stood with both his hands on the open book but with his eyes closed. Ben stopped and frowned.

"How can he read it with his eyes closed?" he asked. Before Ethan could answer, the man seemed to flicker then disappear for a second or so, then he was back again. "What the...?" Ben ex-claimed in surprise. Ethan smothered a smile as Ben turned to his guide. "What just happened?"

"Ah, well, that man is researching another person's life."

"Is that allowed?"

"Oh, yes, it's necessary sometimes. It's called 'merging'."

"Merging? What, you mean he was suddenly in the life he was reading?"

"Sort of," Ethan answered, "only, of course, it's a lot more com-plex than that." He paused trying to think how he could explain it simply but he'd give it a go. "It's like this: there are a couple of reasons why a person may need to merge and the most usual one is to understand the motivation of someone who, in the past, has done something to you, perhaps in a previous existence - especially if in the new life you're planning, there's a chance to meet and settle karmic debts. Understanding brings forgiveness and forgiveness lets you grow and develop, so that's one reason.

"Also, you could re-experience any past life you don't under-stand or, like when you first get here, you review your last lifetime to see the patterns you weren't aware of before. Then there are researchers who wish to experience events in history and they do that by experiencing the lives of people who lived at those times. Haven't you ever wished you could meet a famous historical figure and see what they were really like?"

Ben nodded. "Yes, I have. I always wanted to meet Kit Marlow and ask him what he thought of Shakespeare."

"You're a strange one, Ben," Ethan laughed. "Most people would ask to meet the man himself."

"Oh, I'm sure they would but, for some reason, I've always wanted to meet Marlow."

"Well, up here, you could. But that's not the reason you're here," he added hastily, before Ben could get any ideas. "Anyway, you can access the past, the present and the future of anyone who has ever lived, lives now or will live."

"The future? How is that possible if it hasn't happened yet?"

Ethan groaned as time was the most complicated thing about the universe to explain or even understand. He didn't really know how it worked, he only knew that it did and he'd learned that this was all he needed to know. It saved a few headaches.

"Time is a spiral, not a flat line like we tend to believe on Earth – it's fluid, flexible and flowing. I'm not sure there really is a past, present and future at all, or whether they are all one, or are on different dimensions or planes, whatever." He added with a shrug, "It really doesn't matter how it works as we'll never get our heads round it anyway. All you need to know is that a power far greater than we can ever imagine does understand it and that it works. Believe me, you'll do yourself – and me - a great favour, just to leave if at that."

Ben's head was already spinning, so he just nodded and they continued to walk towards the doors, which opened as they reached them.

CHAPTER 11

A Meeting

They went through the doors onto the top step and both stopped to admire the view. It was only then that Ben noticed the light here was different than on Earth. It was warmer somehow and the sun shone, but it didn't hurt the eyes; the colours were rosier, softer yet fresher too. It was hard to describe but the nearest he could equate it to was the wonderful colours of a sunset, although the sun never set here. He looked to his left and was surprised to see the frontage of another large classical building, which he was sure wasn't there before.

"What's that?" he asked, pointing to it.

"Oh, that's the Hall of Wisdom. It's not included on this tour but when it's time for you to return here at the end of this lifetime, you'll go in there first."

Ethan left it there, not wanting to answer any more questions and began to descend back down the fifty marble steps with Ben trotting after him, swallowing his many questions on what went on in the Hall of Wisdom. Ethan led them past the imposing front portico of the square building with only about ten steps leading to equally magnificent golden doors and marble columns that were spaced out along the front of the building. Once past it, they came to a smaller and completely round, classical building with an elegant domed roof and fine pillars; it too was built in white marble and had steps running all around it.

"And this is?" Ben asked.

"The Hall of Justice," came Ethan's reply. From the way he said it, Ben got the message that they wouldn't be going in there either. Ethan picked up the pace in an attempt to pass the building as quickly as possible, as it stood before the entrance into the gardens that were where Ben was meant to be. To keep up with Ethan, Ben found himself almost running.

"What's the rush?" he panted.

"No rush, I just thought you'd want to see as much as you can."

As they passed the last steps, the Rainbow Gate became visible and Ethan smiled. This place always made him smile, as the memories of the many times he'd found deep joy and serenity inside its boundaries filled a space inside his soul; a space nowhere else could ever fill. He heard a sharp intake of breath behind him and turned to find Ben wide-eyed and open-mouthed, staring transfixed at the shimmering rainbow. Ethan gave him a while to take it in as the beautiful colours and the way it floated in a perfect arch above an ornate, golden garden gate was a breathtaking sight. Ben was, indeed, rendered breathless.

"Oh, goodness… that is…" he managed to utter eventually, and Ethan nodded.

"Yep, this is the Rainbow Gate into the most magical place in the universe - so are you ready to go in?" he asked him. Ben nodded, unable to take his eyes off the rainbow. "Right, come on then," Ethan encouraged, and they walked towards the gate, which once again opened as they got closer to it.

Ben's eyes were still out on stalks as they passed beneath the quivering colours that seemed alive with energy; on the other side, they entered gardens that stretched as far as the eye could see in all directions. How do you ever describe the Gardens of Heaven? Well, you can't, it is impossible to tell another how beautiful they are as words are totally inadequate and there is nowhere on Earth as incredibly wonderful even partly to compare it. The flowers are perfect in every way, from their shapes to their colours and heaven-ly scent, and there are stone pathways, sparkling streams and round, silent, mystic pools of crystal-clear water. Some areas are themed, like the English country garden, the walled Elizabethan garden and the Japanese garden with its precise planting and arranged rocks. The air was filled with a heady scent and the eyes captivated by the harmony of the colours. The birds sing sweetly and butterflies flitter from flower to flower dressed in their brightest colours, adding to the gardens' perfection.

They walked on first through a very formal layout, with small box hedges and artistically arranged flowerbeds, and in the centre was a classical fountain with nymphs and cherubs spurting water out of their mouths. Ben was trailing behind his mentor as they passed between two topiary hedges and then found himself in an avenue of lime trees, whose branches touched to form an archway down which Ethan was already walking, so Ben jogged to catch up with him.

"Where are we going?" he asked again. There did seem to be a destination in mind, as they weren't idly strolling around, admiring the plants.

"I'm going to show you the Towers," he replied. Ben frowned.

"The Towers? Are they gardens?" he queried. Ethan shook his head.

"No, they are buildings here in the gardens, where souls who have been badly traumatised on Earth are brought to heal before they join the rest of us."

"Oh," Ben said, then asked, "How are they traumatised?"

"Many are killed in wars or have been tortured, brainwashed or even murdered, so they're confused and mentally unwell and need a safe place where they can be helped to understand what has happened to them and then let the experience go. They have to detach from the emotions of their time on Earth but still remember the lessons they learned or, maybe, didn't learn."

"Do we all go there when we die?"

"No. It's not necessary for everyone, just those who had problems and illness, like maybe schizophrenia and Alzheimer's."

"What about suicides?"

97

"Yes, those too. They need to be counselled before they can understand the things they did or were done to them, and only then can they start to plan their next incarnation."

"How long does this take?" Ben asked.

"How long is a piece of string?" he shrugged.

"So, as long as it needs to," he smiled, answering his own question. Ethan nodded and returned the smile as it seemed he was catching on fast. They came to the end of the avenue; Ethan pushed open a black, metal gate and went through it into a meadow of grasses and wild flowers. Together they walked up the rise to a ridge where a stand of oak trees stood proud and majestic on the horizon.

As they reached the top, Ben got his first glance of the Towers and, even after all the spectacular sights he'd already seen, he wasn't prepared for them as they eclipsed everything else and made them seem ordinary. They rose elegantly into the sky, two white fairy tale towers that seemed to be made of white marble with blue glass set in it, as if the sky and the stone had merged one inside the other. The light on the glass sent out a blue glow all around, creating a serenity and peace that was exquisite and heavenly.

Ethan had to nudge Ben once again to get his feet moving but slowly, as they got closer, the sound of running water greeted them. For a moment, Ben wasn't sure where it was coming from until he noticed the trickling of water running down some of the white marble walls into scallop-shaped pools, the bowls of which were each painted a different colour, one gold, another purple; he could see a turquoise one and a green one too and, in each, as the water filled them, the colour was released like an energy wave, emitting it into the surrounding area. The whole place vibrated with light, colour, sounds and even scent that came from the jasmine and rose bushes planted everywhere. They stopped again in front of its massive facades and etched, golden doors, marvelling at its beauty.

"It is unreal, almost too perfect," Ben muttered and Ethan smiled.

"Nothing can be too perfect," he commented. But in a way he knew what Ben meant as perfection on Earth didn't exist, though it did here. "Let's take a seat and soak up some of this atmosphere for a while," Ethan said and they found an empty bench and joined all the other souls who were sitting, enjoying the peace of the Towers.

"It seems a popular place," Ben said. Ethan nodded.

"Oh, yes. The Towers and gardens are always busy. It's the energy. Somehow the love feels stronger here than anywhere else so it's the first choice for those who want to relax, meditate or read." Ben looked around at everyone else and found them doing just as Ethan said.

"So, do we meditate?" he asked.

"If you want to. It'll be easier here than on Earth."

"Then I'll give it a go," Ben replied, shutting his eyes. Ethan sat quietly next to him and waited, as he knew that Haniel had guided him here for a reason though that was all he knew.

"And all you need to know," her voice said, and he turned to find her sitting beside him. He was no longer surprised by her sudden appearances but nevertheless was relieved to see her.

"Okay, but what happens next?" he asked.

"A soul is coming to see Ben." Ethan raised an eyebrow.

"A visitor?"

Haniel smiled. "Yes." Then she looked away, sensing the visitor's approach. "And here she is now." Coming towards them was a young woman with dark brown hair that cascaded onto her slim shoulders, framing her oval face and falling in front of her brown eyes. Although he had never met this woman before, Ethan knew who she was.

"Karen," he said and Haniel nodded.

"Yes, it's time for them to talk so that they can resolve this situation and move on, as it is written they must." Ethan nodded and stood up. Karen smiled at them as she arrived and took the seat vacated by Ethan.

"Come now, leave them alone," Haniel said, and together they walked away.

"Will he let her go now?" Ethan asked.

Haniel sighed. "That, as it has always been, is his decision. But I am more confident he will now because of his journey here." Ethan felt good about that; if he had done his bit to help another then this learning experience was worth the growing pains he had suffered. Haniel smiled. "Yes, you have grown," she said before adding, "Yet there is still room for more."

Ethan groaned inwardly. It seemed he'd never finish his work in progress and Haniel silently agreed.

Karen sat silently next to her husband and took a few moments to study him. There were a few more lines around his eyes and some grey in his hair but, other than that, he hadn't changed at all. She loved him but their link to each other was stopping her from planning her next life. Ben's first inkling that it wasn't Ethan sitting next to him anymore came when he smelled a spicy scent he knew all too well; it was Karen's favourite perfume, half a bottle of which he still had and sniffed regularly, every time he remembered her. A smile appeared on his face as he sat there, eyes closed, relaxing in the warm, soft light. Karen smiled too then laid a slender, white hand on his shoulder.

"Ben, we have to talk." At first, he thought he was imagining hearing her voice and feeling her hand until she spoke to him again. "Ben," she said and this time he opened his eyes, though he didn't believe what he was seeing.

"Karen?" he whispered and, with one finger, he touched her cheek, half expecting it to pass right through her. When it didn't, he was shocked. "Karen, is it really you?" he exclaimed.

"Yes, you silly goose, of course it's me."

"I can't believe it. I've wanted to see you again, to hear your voice, for so long."

"I know," she nodded, "but this has got to stop. You know I love you, don't you?" she asked him. He nodded. "And I always will," she continued. "And we will always be linked together on a soul level - we are of the same soul group. But holding on to me so tightly, as Karen, is preventing me from doing what I need to do."

"I know," he sighed. "Kalistra explained it to me but it's just hard to accept that I'll never see you again."

She touched his face. "I know, but my life as Karen is over and it was a wonderful life, full of love and happiness. You gave me so much and I didn't tell you as much as I should have how wonderful you are."

"No, I'm not, I didn't help you enough, I tried to stop you leaving and even now I'm holding on to you. I'm sorry. Can you forgive me?" There were unshed tears in his eyes and she felt his pain, his guilt, like a palpable force.

"Oh, my love, there's nothing to forgive. You supported me, cared for me, loved and cherished me - what more could I ask for? But now you need to find love again. You are still young with many years to look forward to, so please, Ben, promise me you'll not spend them all alone." He looked down and took her hand before he answered.

"If that's what you want."

"I want you to be happy, to have the children we so longed for, and not to feel guilty about laughing and having fun."

He looked at her sharply. "How did you know?" he asked, surprised by her words, which described how he had been feeling lately.

"Because I am and always will be connected to you and soul groups always know how each member is, whether they're in the spirit world or on Earth."

"Soul groups?" he asked.

"Yes, every soul belongs to a group. We usually incarnate together, to help each other to learn certain lessons. It's a bit like a large family really. Some members are on Earth, some here, but you always recognise your soul group even if they are in unfamiliar bodies."

"Is that why we immediately got on together when we first met?" he asked, remembering how easy he had found it talking to her when he was normally so tongue-tied and awkward with women, especially pretty ones.

"Yes, and we shall meet again in another time and place or here in spirit. So you are not losing me forever, it's not 'goodbye', more like 'see you soon'." He smiled at that, as it had always been Karen's way never to say goodbye; even when she was dying in his arms, she had whispered "Ciao" before she died, a smile still on her lips. He knew now that he could finally let her go, especially as it wasn't forever and he had felt her love once more.

"I do love you," he said.

"And I love you. And you have nothing to feel guilty about, so please live the life you were meant to live, then I can be free too." He nodded.

"Yes, I will, and thank you for everything."

"Ditto," she laughed, and kissed him on the lips. He closed his eyes to savour the moment, then she was gone and all that was left was the scent of her perfume.

CHAPTER 12

The Indigo Child

Ethan saw Karen kiss Ben and then disappear. They looked so happy together but hopefully they had resolved their problems now and would move on. He turned to Haniel.

"Do I take him back now?"

"Yes, it is time," she nodded.

"Will he remember all of this when he wakes up?" Ethan enquired, as he knew how quickly dreams fade from the memory when you awake. Haniel smiled.

"Oh, he'll remember all right. Don't worry, this experience isn't a dream so it will not fade and disappear. He now has the information he needs to live his life to his highest spiritual potential. All he has to do is choose to live it." Ethan grimaced, as that word 'choice' was becoming a bit annoying. Haniel knew what he was thinking and laughed. "Oh, Ethan, you are so funny," she said, giving him the feeling that he was just on this project for her entertainment and amusement. She patted his shoulder. "No, you're here to learn," she said, then added, "but you are amusing." With that, she too vanished before he could think of a suitable retort. He shook his head and muttered "Angels!" in exasperation.

Ben got up from the bench and walked over to Ethan.

"Are you okay?" Ethan asked him. Ben smiled sadly but nodded.

"Yes, I'm okay. It's not easy to let her go but I will for her sake and mine." Ethan was glad, for at least he'd helped him to realise that he couldn't live in the past.

"Well, that's good," he said. "It's time now for you to go back to Earth."

"I'm ready. But I have one question for you first."

"What's that?"

"I'm worried that I'll forget all I've seen and learned when I get back."

Ethan laughed and answered, "Don't worry, I have it on good authority that you'll remember every syllable, every word. You have been given a great gift."

Ben agreed. "Yes, I know. And finally I see a path that I can and will follow, a way to live a fulfilled life and help others like I was supposed to. No, I'm not going to screw it up again - this time, I'll do it right." Ethan believed him.

"That's good, my friend," he said, "then my work is done." He led Ben out of the gardens and under the Rainbow Arch to the top of the vortex. "Take my hand and in a moment you'll be back in your body, waking to a new day."

"The first day of the rest of my life," Ben added.

Ethan smiled. "Exactly," he said, as they stepped into the vortex and back to Earth. Haniel was already waiting for their arrival and, as they emerged from the tunnel, Ethan said his goodbyes. "Well, pal, I hope you find everything you're looking for."

Ben nodded. "I will, now I know what I want."

"That always helps, doesn't it?" Ethan agreed.

"Yes, it does," Ben smiled. He looked down at his sleeping body and added, "So, how do I get in there?"

"Easy. Just think yourself there and you'll do it - you've done it many times before." Ben frowned, remembering something.

"Is that when you feel like you're falling and you jerk yourself awake?" he asked.

"Yep, it can be, but you can do it a lot smoother than that. Just don't think about it and you will slip in like a greased pig in a poke."

Ben's eyebrows rose at that but he didn't comment.

"Well, thank you for your guidance."

"My pleasure," Ethan said and they shook hands. "Now scoot," Ethan said and waved his hands at him. Ben smiled, then turned away to face his own body; it was so strange to look down on it like this and really not have any great attachment to it. But there was no longer any reason to stay out of it, so he took a deep breath and decided to close his eyes to make it easier to slip into the shell.

With fingers crossed, he said to himself, 'I'm now inside my body and I will remember everything that I've heard and seen.' Slowly and gently, his essence slipped easily back inside the physical vehicle that was, this time around, Ben Harris, and he woke up.

Ethan joined Haniel in a corner of the room and asked, "He is going to be all right now, isn't he?"

"Nothing's written in stone," she smiled, "but, yes, I'd say he is."

"Good."

Down on Earth, seven-year old Jason sat on his bed with the framed photograph of him and his beloved Granddad Tom on their camping trip in his hands and tried not to cry, but he couldn't help it. In one day his whole world had changed and he didn't know what to do; all he knew for sure was that he wanted to see Granddad Tom again, if only to say goodbye. But his Mum had told him this was impossible because he was now in Heaven with the angels. Jason sniffed and wiped the tears out of his blue eyes, annoyed by this; he was sure the angels could get on with whatever they did without his granddad's help, whereas he needed him here.

They were pals and spent so much time together, especially since his dad never had time for him and was always going away on business. Granddad Tom took him for walks in the woods and showed him secret things, like where the badgers live, and he'd been going to take him there one evening to see them feeding. But now he was gone and Jason felt so alone without him to talk to.

"Why did you leave me, Granddad?" he shouted, and then the tears began again and he felt like his heart was breaking. He didn't think anyone cared, but he was wrong. His guide looked down on the small boy with straw blond wavy hair, dressed in his Superman pyjamas and with tears streaming down his rounded cheeks, the picture of misery, and knew the boy needed more help than he could give him. He needed divine help, so he put out a call to the angels and hoped Jason would get lucky.

Haniel indicated that it was time for them to leave and together they returned to the round chamber overlooking the Earth. Ethan was happy to sink down onto a cool, marble bench and rest, as it was tiring doing this guiding work. Haniel joined him and, for a few precious moments, they sat together in silent companionship; although Ethan knew this peaceful interlude wouldn't last long, he intended to enjoy it. His eyes were drawn, as always, to the beauty of the Earth as it spun majestically below them, with the weather systems that went around the planet easy to see from this vantage point. The areas of swirling, white clouds, streaming across the Atlantic, bringing rain to the Emerald Isle, were visible, as was the sparkle of sunlight on the vast body of ocean water that shimmered and glittered, sending slithers of light back up into the sky. It was a beautiful sight, an ever-changing panorama, and one he'd never tired of seeing. The Atlantic slipped by and the Americas came into view. He was shocked by just how built-up the eastern seaboard had become, with its accompanying mushroom of pollution and dirty shoreline. It pained him to see it. Earth was such a precious jewel, with such a diversity of wildlife and habitations able to support an endless variety of life, but its abundance wasn't unlimited; only Man seems to believe so.

Haniel understood his pain and although she had never lived on Earth she knew how important it was, not just as a learning school for human souls but as a place where so many other soul groups could develop. Whether mankind made the transition to a higher spiritual level was very much in their own hands - and in the hands of souls like Ethan who would be guiding tomorrow's children, the new souls charged with bringing love and wisdom to the planet.

Since the 1960s, souls had been incarnating with the desire to conserve, to protect and to honour the planet. Then a new wave of children who are destined to work with Earth, the indigo children, were born in the 1980s followed by children of the new millennium who were highly developed souls, incarnating to bring love back into human consciousness with the hope that the future could be so much better. Hope is a word with such power and forgiveness, the only way forward, for a soul that holds onto hate and anger never moves on and condemns itself to the darkness. The human race had to change and change always starts with the children.

One such child had come to Haniel's attention. Jason may have been seven but his soul was much older than that, a special child who had chosen to return to Earth with a special task to do. The loss of his beloved grandfather Tom, who had been instrumental in mentoring him, had hit Jason very hard and since his death Jason's deepest wish was to see him once more and say goodbye, as he had been prevented from visiting Tom in hospital. Every night, he knelt down by his bed and asked, in his prayers, to have his wish granted. Haniel had been alerted by Jason's gatekeeper, who thought he might qualify for some divine intervention.

Haniel had to agree, so Jason was to get some help with his wish. At first, she had leaned towards bringing Tom back from the other side to see his grandson. This had been the plan, but two new elements had appeared to make her reconsider. The first concerned Jason and his own soul path. She had taken a look at his Akashic record for this lifetime and realised just how special a little boy he was, with important global work to accomplish; but the loss of his grandfather could very easily steer him off his true path and he might never find it again. There were other people of influence in his life who might persuade him to pursue a different path, which would cause ripples in the cosmos that might become waves; she didn't think this was a good outcome for either Jason or the planet. Then in came Ethan, the second element, and she smiled to herself; maybe element number two could help element number one and come up with a result with which everyone would be happy. All she had to do now was to convince Ethan that Jason should be his last chosen person, and that should be a piece of cake for an archangel.

"Well, Ethan, you've helped Kathleen find peace and Ben his purpose, so you should be quite pleased with yourself." He frowned, wary about the potential of a hidden meaning to her complimentary words as, once bitten, he was a lot more cautious before he opened his big mouth and put his foot firmly in it. But finally he worked out a reply with which he could live.

"I'm happy to have been able to give them a chance to find their own answers, but I don't think I did very much."

He was right, of course, but essentially that was exactly what guides were supposed to do: show their charges a different way of looking at things. It is a guide's duty to open up their tunnel vision so that they can see the bigger picture, to understand that they have many choices and then, hopefully, find the right one for them. Ethan was now beginning to be able to facilitate without giving an opinion, since his opinion wasn't relevant to another person's life, but it was hard for new guides to step back and allow others to make what they could see might be the wrong choice. There is no absolute right or absolute wrong choice; it's all a matter of timing and circumstances. Guides do not tell their charges to do anything; that was the cardinal rule, the big no-no, the most important prime directive the Creator had ever given. Haniel believed that Ethan would be perfect for the role and this experience was definitely helping him know what he'd be letting himself in for.

"You are right, Ethan, you did enough and that is the trick - they help themselves. So, who gets your assistance now?" she asked. He shook his head.

"I don't know. Do you have anyone in mind?" He had his tongue firmly in his cheek as he said that, having got the feeling he was being set up for each of his recipients. She had said when they'd started this process that the most needy souls would find him and he'd know immediately who they were. Even he couldn't have missed Kathleen's cries though he wasn't so sure about Ben; he tended to believe that Haniel had more than a hand in that choice. Now the final recipient was about to be chosen. Was he or Haniel going to find them or had she already, as he suspected, made the choice? She knew what he was thinking and was impressed that he'd figured this out.

"I must confess," she laughed, "that I do have a young person who is very special and could do with a trip to Heaven."

"Another day tripper?" he asked, a small smile hovering around his lips.

"Mmm, something like that."

Ethan got up and walked around the circular room, thinking hard. Should be take the bait or look for someone by himself? So far, it seemed to him, he hadn't chosen anyone, but maybe that was the point since, when he was to become someone's guide, would he get any say in who that was? He frowned. Perhaps he should ask about that, so he moved back to Haniel.

"Can I ask you a question?" She nodded and let him ask it, even though she knew what it was. "Do I have a choice about the soul I'm to guide, or am I just assigned to someone?"

She shook her head. "You are not given to someone like some package. You would be assigned to one of your soul group who is preparing to reincarnate."

"So, I'll know them?"

"Yes, you will, and you'll probably have lived at least one lifetime with them. He or she won't be a perfect stranger."

"Oh," he said and sat down again to digest what she'd told him. He was glad that he would have some connection with the soul entrusted to him; it might make it easier to communicate - but then again it might not. This whole guiding thing filled him alternately with excitement and terror and he still wasn't sure he was up to the job. A hand gently touched his shoulder.

"You are, you know," Haniel said, reassuringly.

He wanted to believe her but inside there was still a kernel of doubt. Still, in a split second, he had made up his mind that this young person Haniel had picked out was going to get his or her day trip. He really couldn't turn down an archangel's choice anyway, and if she believed he was special and need a helping hand right now, how could he refuse?

"I'll take you to see him in a moment, but first I'll tell you just a little about him and why he needs to come here." She paused briefly before continuing. "His name is Jason and he's seven years old."

"Only seven?" exclaimed Ethan. "Won't he be scared of me?"

"Who'd be scared of you," she laughed, "with such an angelic face?" He scowled at that as it had been said before and he didn't much like it, but she pinched his cheeks playfully and carried on. "Now, Jason is a child with a global mission."

"Global? Wow, that's tough," Ethan commented.

"Yes, it is, but he is a very advanced soul, one that didn't need to return to Earth but chose to, to take on this mission. He is one of many special children who have been born recently. As you now know, everyone has a destiny: his is to raise awareness of the danger humans are in because of how they treat the Earth. Of course, everyone has free will that can lead them astray so that their potential and life-goals are never realised."

"So, is that the problem?"

She shook her head. "No, he is a very strong-willed, determined little boy, but he has just lost a very important person in his life, his grandfather."

"Oh," Ethan said. He knew how hard that could be, as in one of his own lives he had been orphaned and then raised by his grandfather; his loss had overshadowed the rest of that lifetime. Haniel smiled, knowing all about Ethan's lives, which was why she believed he would be the right person to help Jason. He would understand and be empathic but hopefully remain detached, as a good guide should be, and it would be another challenge on the long road to enlightenment.

"Jason's grandfather was also an evolved soul who had taken on the role as guide and mentor to Jason. He took him out into the countryside and taught him the importance of the natural world, which is where Jason's destiny lies. He will be a very effective champion for Mother Earth if he stays on his soul path."

"Then what's the problem? He seems to have his way prepared," Ethan frowned. Somehow, he wasn't getting the whole story.

"Life is never as easy as that. It is not black and white, right or wrong or even good and bad. There are many traps for the unwary and even when you know what your life's purpose is, often, even then, it isn't easy to follow or achieve."

"Yet so many people say it is, don't they?" he commented, having gone through this very process on his last incarnation. He had found what he knew in his heart was his life's path yet had kept running into brick walls; all his friends said that if it truly was his life's work then it would all fall into place and be easy so, as it wasn't, then he must be mistaken. Although he'd heard that so often, he couldn't give up his hope, his faith that he was on the right track even if it was still a struggle. Then just as he felt he couldn't go on any longer, something happened. It was as if all the pieces of the jigsaw fell into place at once and suddenly he got the help he needed, the right people appeared as if by magic at the right time and he moved easily and effortlessly forward. He felt like the universe had wanted to see if he were truly committed to the path he was taking and, when he proved that he was, the help he needed had arrived.

"Yes," Haniel agreed, "help will come but not always in the form one imagines it will. It's like the story of the man in the flood." Ethan frowned; he wasn't sure he knew the story that she was referring to and, on seeing his expression, she laughed. "You must know it, Ethan," she chided.

"I'm not sure - why don't you tell me?"

"Okay, if I must, but I'm positive you know it." She paused, then said, "There was a flood and a devout man sat on his house roof, waiting to be rescued. He prayed to God, asking Him to save him. Just then a man in a boat came by and offered to row him to higher ground. 'No thank you,' said the man, 'I'm waiting for God to save me.' So the man in the boat went on. Later a helicopter came by and dropped a ladder for the man to climb on board, but again he refused, saying God would save him." She saw Ethan's face clearing; he had heard it before. "Why don't you tell me the rest?"

"All right. The water got higher and the man drowned. When he got to Heaven he said to God, 'Why didn't you save me?' and God said, 'I sent you a boat and a helicopter, why didn't you use them?' He'd been expecting help in some sort of divine flash or something so, instead of seeing help in the obvious way right in front of him, he ignored it and drowned."

"That's it," she nodded, "the obvious seems to be too obvious for some people on Earth to grasp."

They sat quietly together, watching the Earth slowly rotate before them, both thinking how life on the planet was so different and unclear, unlike in spirit, not an easy option at all. Just remembering one's life's goals once incarnate was very difficult and could lead one up many a wrong path before, if you were lucky, you stumbled on the right one; but the problems didn't always end there, as Ethan was all too aware. Sometimes he wondered why any soul in its right mind would put itself through the same problems again and again. He smiled at that thought, as he had, hadn't he? It certainly looked a whole lot easier when you planned your life with your guide. You knew exactly the challenges you were going to meet, the other souls with whom you had issues and your life's purpose, as it was all laid out in front of you. Go to A then walk the line to B where you meet C and so on, like the script of a movie.

The only problem was that once you were on Earth you couldn't remember any of it and you were as blind as the proverbial bat. It could take more than half one's lifetime to start on the true path and begin to know what life was all about. Of course, some never do figure it out at all. Haniel sympathised but she also knew that if souls had access to their 'script' before they were ready, it could present more problems than it solved. The Creator made it the way it is for a reason and who could know better? Haniel patted Ethan's arm and decided it was time they got back on track and talked about Jason and the reason he needed his day trip to Heaven.

CHAPTER 13

Adventure

"Jason is a strong young man," Haniel continued, "but he is, as you so rightly pointed out, only seven. Tom was a great influence on him but sadly his death has left Jason very low and vulnerable. There are other forces at work around him that would very much like to steer him off his true path and onto one where his power would be neutralised." Ethan frowned as he'd never heard her talk like this before; it sounded more like the planning of a military campaign than a little boy's life.

"Neutralised?" he asked.

She nodded, her lips pressed together in a thin line and her eyes shining with a deep passion; she was kind of scary-looking, not at all what he'd grown used to. This was the side of angelic power he'd never witnessed before, the defender of the innocent and protector of the weak. He'd heard stories of Michael with his huge sword in hand, scaring the living daylights out of the wayward and bringing them firmly back into line, but he'd never have believed that dear, gentle Haniel could do it too. He swallowed once and waited for her reply.

"Yes, they will try to stop him and that cannot be tolerated. He must be left to follow his heart - whether or not he chooses to take up his mission, it still must be his choice." Her voice rose as she spoke those final words and he got the message. For a few seconds, she remained very erect and full of vibrant power, then she smiled down at him. "You see, Ethan, there are those who work for the shadow side, who want others to fail, and around Jason there are two such beings who have noticed his potential and want to stop his progress."

"And going up to Heaven will prevent this?"

"Maybe," she shrugged, "and maybe not, but the odds increase in his favour. As I keep saying, it is in his hands, as young as he is. The main benefit of his trip will be to reunite him with Granddad Tom and it is then up to him to give Jason some guidance."

Ethan sighed. It appeared he was just going to be the tour guide again.

"But you are so good at it," she said, laughing at his pained expression and squeezing his arm. "Haven't you learned anything from helping the others?" He nodded.

"Of course I have."

"And you will again. Trust me, I'm -"

"- an angel," he finished it for her.

A small figure sat on the grass, his arms around his calves, chin resting on bent knees, gazing into the distance and feeling very alone even though his parents and younger sister were with him. They were playing with a ball and laughing, enjoying the sunshine and fresh air, whereas Jason just felt cold with an empty space inside him that nothing seemed to fill. He knew his father was beginning to lose patience with him and numerous times he had been told to pull himself together and get on with living, but without Granddad Tom the world had lost all its magic. Somehow Jason had always known he was different from the rest of his family and Granddad Tom seemed to recognise it too. They had a special bond, a way of being that didn't need the spoken word; it was just there and the adventures they had experienced just deepened it.

"Why did you leave me alone, Granddad?" he whispered as a large tear ran down the side of his face.

He had to hide his tears now as, six months after Tom's death was considered by his father at least long enough to grieve. Jason was expected to forget his loss and carry on as if nothing dreadful had happened; he had tried but his heart wasn't in it. So he grieved alone and had become withdrawn and very unhappy. Ethan looked at the sad little boy and remembered pain like that and the lack of understanding by those who should know better. Grief is a very personal thing. Everyone is different; some can grieve right away, letting their feelings out and releasing the pain, while others hold it in for years before finally it breaks out in a tide of emotion that can overwhelm them, which really isn't the healthiest way. Grief doesn't have a timetable, it isn't regulated or controlled, but is unpredictable and immeasurable. Telling someone to stop grieving is like telling them to stop feeling; it's impossible, insulting and intolerant.

The human race seemed to be in such a hurry nowadays, thought Ethan; even death had to be recovered from in double-quick time so that other, supposedly more important things could be returned to, another case of the lack of love, tolerance and understanding that ruled the Earth now. Haniel looked at the scene and she too was saddened that Jason had chosen to incarnate with his father, who had a problem with his need to control others, especially family members, and with his volatile temper. These were the actions of a young soul, one who has yet to learn that being human often means you have little control over anything, especially others. It wasn't going to be easy for Jason to stay on his chosen course with such a parent, who had already decided that his son was going to be a banker, preferably a very rich one.

Tom's influence would have been invaluable to Jason but it had been decided that, when the boy turned seven, Tom would return to spirit. Although this didn't mean he was abandoning Jason, it meant that the relationship was to move to another level; and just because Tom was no longer in physical form, it didn't mean he'd stopped loving Jason or wanting to help and support him. All Jason needed to do was learn how he could communicate with this grandfather in the heavenly realm and Ethan's task was to take Jason and show him how close Heaven really is. Often it has been said that there is only a thin veil between Heaven and Earth and this is true, but without the right intention or pure heart it is as stout as a stone wall; whereas for others who have the key, it is transparent as gossamer and like having the password for a computer.

Haniel tapped Ethan on the shoulder and, when he turned to look up at her, she said, "Well, you can see that Jason has a problem."

"His father?"

"Yes, he will try to pull Jason off his soul path."

"And will he be able to?"

"That is a possibility…" she paused, "although, with your help, he might be able to resist the attempts to divert him." Ethan wasn't so sure that he was the one who could help; that was more likely to be Tom's job.

"If it is so essential that he stays on his chosen path, then why did Tom die? Surely, his help and support were too important, to lose?"

"You're still thinking in small terms, aren't you?"

"Am I?"

"Yes you are. Look, in the cosmos all beings interconnect with each other, in spirit worlds and on Earth. You must think of Earth life as a play - as Shakespeare said, 'The world is but a stage…' Some players take their leave at what might seem to others the wrong time."

"Like Tom?"

"Yes, but it wasn't the wrong time for him, it was exactly the right time."

"And was it the right time for Jason?"

"Yes, although he doesn't see it like that at the moment. But he must learn to be strong."

"And if I take him to Heaven, will Tom be able to keep him on his path?"

"I believe so. At least he will be able to teach Jason how to communicate with him, so he won't feel isolated. Then Tom's help will be always available to him and that alone could keep him on track. I think we've talked enough - now it's time to act."

Ethan raised an eyebrow. "And how exactly do we do that?"

"You ask Jason if he'd like to see Tom in Heaven."

"Oh, easy then," Ethan exclaimed.

"Yes, it is. Take my hand and I'll show you." He took hold of her offered hand and suddenly found himself standing on the grass in front of the seated little boy.

Jason shivered as a shadow fell across him, dropping the temperature several degrees; he looked up and was surprised to find a man standing over him. At first, he couldn't make out his face as the light was behind him, making his features dark and undefined, but then the man crouched down so they were on the same level and he could see his face. It was a friendly one with large, brown, oval eyes, a neat nose and wide lips that, when he smiled, showed regular white teeth. His hair was brown and longer than most grown-ups Jason knew and his clothes were unusual too.

"Hello, Jason," the man said in a soft voice.

"You know my name?" Jason gasped.

"Yes, I do," Ethan nodded. "Do you want to know how?" Jason did but he was also a bit worried. He glanced over at his parents, who hadn't seemed to have noticed this strange man, before he turned back.

"I'm not supposed to speak to strangers."

"That's good, you shouldn't, but I'm not really a stranger," Ethan grinned.

"But I don't know you."

"No, you're right again, you don't. But you've been asking for help, haven't you? And I've been sent to help you."

Jason's frown deepened. "I did?"

"Yes, in your prayers. Do you remember you asked God for something?" Jason did know and he nodded.

"Yes, to see Granddad Tom," he whispered. "But Daddy says I can't, he's in Heaven."

"That he is, but if you want to I can take you there, so you can see him again."

Jason gasped, his large blue eyes wide open in astonishment. "You can?" he whispered and Ethan nodded. "I do want to see him but Daddy will say 'No'," the boy said miserably, looking down.

"Ah, but they won't even know."

Jason looked up in hope and surprise. He was tempted, but how could he go without his parents finding out? Ethan guessed what he was thinking and decided that an explanation was called for.

"You want to come, don't you?" he asked and Jason nodded. "But you're scared your parents won't let you."

"They won't," Jason said dejectedly, a glint of moisture appearing around his eyes.

"What if I show you how you can come up to Heaven with me and they'll never ever know about it? It'll be like a time travel adventure."

Jason's eyes opened wide. "Wow, really? Time travel?"

"Yes, time travel. What that means is we go up to Heaven but no time will pass on Earth while we're gone. So when we come back it will be as if it's only a second after we left." Jason frowned and Ethan gave him a minute or two to think about it. The boy wasn't sure he understood but all he really wanted was to see Tom.

"Then I'll see Granddad Tom?" he asked.

"That's right, kiddo."

Just then, Jason's father walked towards them. "Come and play with your sister, Jason," he said loudly. Jason sat up in surprise, as his father hadn't said anything about the stranger; he was totally ignoring the man as if he couldn't see him. Ethan smiled.

"That's right, he can't see me," he said and waved mischievously at Jason's dad.

"Jason, I'm talking to you. Are you listening?" Jason found it hard to keep a straight face, as his new friend made silly faces at his father who was totally oblivious to him.

Somehow, he managed to say, "I'm okay here, Dad."

"But you've been sat down all afternoon. Well, your mother's going to start getting our picnic out soon so I'll come and get you then." He turned away and left them in peace. Once he was far enough not to overhear him, Jason turned to Ethan.

"He really didn't see you."

"I know, fun isn't it?"

"Yes, I wish I could be invisible," Jason giggled.

"Ah well, you can with a little help. Would you like that?" The boy nodded, not quite sure he was hearing right. "Okay, so are you going to come with me to see Tom?" Ethan asked. Jason nodded.

"I'm coming," he said, firmly.

"Good, well this is what we do. You hold my hand and close your eyes for a moment and, when I tell you, you can open them again and you'll be invisible."

"Cool," Jason said in wonder and held out his hand eagerly.

Ethan took it then added, "Oh, and you'll not be in your body, because that has to stay here so your parents won't know you've gone." Jason accepted that completely, merely nodding his understanding. Ethan smiled. Sometimes children were a lot easier to deal with than adults, they didn't ask those hard-to-answer questions but just accepted things as they are. He looked at his eager companion's upturned face. "Close your eyes and count to ten."

Jason took a deep breath and began counting but before he'd got to six he was out of his body, standing next to Ethan in his etheric form. Ethan waited 'til he reached ten.

"Open your eyes."

Jason did so and smiled. It didn't bother him much at all that he was standing next to his new friend while also still sitting on the grass, except there was one thing that worried him.

"How long will we be? Mummy will call me soon for my tea."

"Oh, you'll be back before that," Ethan said confidently, but

Jason's face fell at this news. Ethan frowned; he wasn't sure what was wrong but something definitely was. "Hey, what's up?" he asked.

"Nothing," Jason muttered, looking at his etheric feet.

"Hmm, I beg to differ," Ethan stated and he crouched down so he was eyeball to eyeball with his youngest winner. He placed his hand under Jason's chin and tilted his head up so they were facing each other. "Okay then, friends can tell each other when something's wrong, can't they? So, kiddo, what's up? Don't you want to come now?"

"Oh no, I really want to come, only, it won't be long enough." Jason looked down again to cover the tears in his eyes and Ethan frowned for a moment, trying to work out what he meant. Then it dawned on him.

"Oh, I see," he said, "You think we'll only be up in Heaven for a few minutes." Jason looked up at him and nodded and Ethan laughed. "I'm sorry, I should have explained it better. Time in Heaven isn't like on Earth. We might be there for hours, even days, but only a moment will have passed down here." Jason considered this and gradually a small smile returned to his face.

"Oh, that's all right then 'cause Mummy will be ready soon." They both looked over to where Jason's mother was busily laying out the food she'd prepared on a chequered rug. It looked good. Ethan reluctantly looked away from the mountain of delicacies and back to his charge.

"Yes, well I guess we'd better be going then," he said. Jason smiled and opened his mouth to say something and stopped, frowning.

"What's your name?" he asked. Ethan was stunned for a second as he couldn't believe he hadn't introduced himself.

"I'm sorry, young man," he said and held out his right hand to be shaken. "I'm Ethan, your tour guide for this day trip to Heaven." Jason solemnly shook his hand.

"Pleased to meet you," he said in a very grownup voice. Ethan smiled and stood up, taking Jason by the hand.

"Now it's time to get this show on the road."

With that, a vortex appeared in front of them and with a look of reassurance Ethan led Jason towards it and stepped inside. They were gently sucked up a tunnel-like structure towards a golden light that seemed a long way away.

"Wow," Jason said. Ethan always enjoyed this experience and it would appear he wasn't the only one. It didn't take long to reach their destination and they stepped out of the vortex into the brightest light ever imagined. Ethan looked at his companion.

"We've arrived," he said and began to walk with Jason tagging along, trying to see things but the light was too bright for him to make out anything.

"Is this Heaven?" he asked, as it certainly wasn't what he expected.

"Yep, only we're not quite there yet," Ethan answered.

They kept on walking until finally the light dimmed and colours other than gold could be seen; they had entered what looked like a country lane with grassy banks and hedgerows on each side. Wild flowers of many different colours grew under the hedges, making intricate coloured patterns interwoven with the green of the grass. In the distance Jason thought he could make out a gate, an ornate, black metal one. Ethan wondered why Haniel had sent them to one of the side gates into the Tower Gardens. Maybe Jason wasn't supposed to see the Halls of Justice, Wisdom or Records just yet.

"Are we there yet?" the boy asked, plaintively.

"Nearly," Ethan replied, and a few moments later they were leaning on the gate, looking into the formal Rose Garden. The scent could only be described as heavenly, coming from the huge roses that were planted in carefully cut beds that had been planted to make a spectacular visual impact. With the blending of their perfectly executed vibrant colours and a mix of standard, climbing and rambling roses, it was perfect. There were gold, orange, peach and yellow roses in one bed that gently merged into cream and apricot ones in a symphony of harmony. There were no diseases or blight in these gardens and every flower was bigger, bolder and more magnificent than on Earth. Ethan had always loved the scent of roses, so he took the time to stand, leaning on the gate, breathing in the sight and smell of them. Jason's eyes were wide open. Granddad Tom loved roses and had grown them in his small back garden, but they had never looked like these.

"Big," he said eventually and Ethan nodded.

"They are, aren't they? Bet you've never seen any as beautiful as these before?" Jason looked around at the many beds and multitude of colours and shook his head.

"No, I haven't. Did the angels make them?" Ethan laughed as that was a first for him. He'd heard the angels getting the credit for a lot of things but not for the roses before.

"No, God did that. Come on, let's have a look around." Jason followed him and they wandered in companionable silence, looking at the flowers, stopping to smell some and to appreciate the beauty of the others. Ethan wasn't quite sure what he was supposed to do now, as Haniel hadn't told him very much except to encourage Jason to make the trip. Well, he had accomplished that, so where now?

"Go to the Japanese Garden," Haniel's voice said in his ear. Although he couldn't see her, her presence was felt. He nodded and began to walk slowly towards the northern end of the Rose Garden to where some high hedges bordered it; in the corner was an arched opening into the next garden, an English border garden that led onto the stylised Japanese one. Jason followed along behind, humming softly to himself quite happily, not in the least concerned by the fact that he was only in his etheric body while in Heaven. Ethan hadn't had it this easy before, as both Kathleen and Ben had been apprehensive and unsure of what might happen on this side of the veil. Jason, in contrast, didn't have a care in the world. Like most children, he was enjoying the moment, not obsessed with the future or the feeling guilty about the past.

The borders were deep and planted in a graduated fashion with the smallest plants at the front and the tallest at the back, a very pleasing arrangement both visually and aromatically. Here, the colours ranged from hot reds and oranges to cooler violets and blues into the white border, which was only punctuated by the green of the foliage. Ethan hadn't been a keen gardener in his past life but he always appreciated the skill and dedication it took to create something this beautiful; the only difference between Heaven and Earth was the scale and harmony. Here, there was no need for weed killers or even gardeners and the Creator's best work was on show for all to appreciate and enjoy.

As they reached the end of the long borders, Ethan wondered what awaited them on the other side as he glanced down at Jason. He was such a small, fragile-looking boy but he was happily skipping along the path with a huge smile on his face. They rounded a bend and up in front of them they could see two large stone stylised lions and behind them were two red pillars, supporting a red crossbar, a stark red square entrance into a Japanese garden of great peace and simplicity. Although the style of gardening was very different from the colourful English gardens that had gone before it, in its own way it was just as pleasing.

They moved slowly down the neatly raked gravel paths, following the sound of tinkling water and rounded a corner that opened onto a vista of multi-coloured azaleas and rhododendrons. Vivid oranges sat happily next to purples and reds without clashing or disharmony.

"Wow," Jason said, as they stopped in their tracks to stare at the rainbow before them.

★

CHAPTER 14

An Unexpected Conversation

Ethan understood the boy's expression of astonishment as he still felt that jolt of amazement at the intensity of the colours in Heaven. He let him take his time drinking it all in before gently guiding him down the path that wound its way amongst them. The rhododendrons formed a beautiful hedge as they walked on, the sound of running water getting stronger all the time, and another bend revealed a tranquil lake with a small island in the middle. There sat a small Shinto temple and an elegantly shaped cherry tree covered with pink blossom. A small humped, stone bridge connected the island to the path, guarded by two statues of some mythical creatures made of bronze with fierce expressions on their faces. Jason patted them and giggled.

"They're funny," he said.

Ethan didn't think they were supposed to be but had to admit that the exaggerated fierceness was comical. Then just as they were about to move on, a movement inside the temple caught Ethan's eye. He stopped in mid-stride and looked again - there it was again, a shadow upon the white, paper walls. Was this Tom, although it didn't look human? In two minds what to do, they both hesitated, looking towards the temple, when suddenly one of the paper panels creaked open and the head of a deer popped out. It looked right at them as they stared with mouths open, then it fully emerged from the paper and trotted towards them, quite unafraid. Jason gasped and moved instinctively behind Ethan, who smiled to himself as the deer stopped in front of the guide and looked around him straight at Jason.

"I won't hurt you," it said.

Jason gasped again and tugged Ethan's clothes. "It spoke," he whispered. Ethan looked down at him and nodded.

"They can up here," he said.

"Oh!" Jason exclaimed in surprise.

"Aren't you going to speak to me?" the deer said.

Jason gulped once, pulled himself up to his full height and said, "Yes, I am…" He didn't quite know what else to say and the deer sighed.

"I was hoping you were going to help us."

Jason frowned. "Help you?" he asked.

"That's right. Don't you remember what you promised to do on Earth before you went there?"

Ethan had the feeling that the hand of a certain archangel was firmly behind this encounter and subtlety was obviously not on the cards for Jason. He heard a faint laugh and knew he was right: poor Jason was going to get the message of his intended life purpose whether he liked it or not. This visit may be to meet Tom, but that wasn't by any means the only reason for it and he felt he'd been just a little bit used again. But why be surprised? Jason edged cautiously around Ethan's legs and gazed transfixed at the deer, who gazed back; its ability to talk seemed to render Jason speechless, and he still hadn't answered the question. So it was asked again.

"Do you remember that you wanted to be able to help the world's creatures?" Jason nodded hesitantly. "So, have you changed your mind?" Jason shook his head. "But you might be persuaded by others to do something different?"

Jason frowned at this. He didn't know, though he did feel his father's heavy hand on his shoulder sometimes and, since Tom died, his trips out into nature, walking and bird-watching, had ceased. When he'd asked why, his father had told him they were a waste of time that should be spending mastering his computer or doing more homework. He could hear his voice now, saying, "If you don't learn your times tables, you won't be able to be a banker." Jason wasn't sure what a banker was but he had a feeling that he didn't want to be one.

Tom had never really got on with Jason's father. He hadn't wanted his daughter to marry a man with so little comprehension or feeling for the natural world. Gerry Rice was only really interested in one thing and that was money and how he could get more of it, and he judged people by the size of their pay packets and the status of their jobs; this was always the first thing he tried to find out whenever he met someone new. Tom, on the other hand, believed that what you did spoke volumes and it wasn't about money; that wasn't very important to him, it was how you lived. Did you respect others, not just the people you judged were on equal terms with you but also those less fortunate than yourself? But it went deeper than that; he respected the land, the water, the air and the plants and all the creatures on the planet, and he'd tried to instil this into Jason. Not that it was hard, as Jason loved all these just as much as Tom did. He was nothing like his father, much to Tom's relief, and Tom had taken the time to show Jason as much as he could. They'd walked for hours in the local woods, looking closely at the natural world and Jason would always remember these times together.

The deer gently nudged Jason once to remind him that he hadn't responded to his last question. Jason wiped a tear from his eye as he thought of his beloved grandfather, then sighed heavily once and raised his eyes to look at the deer.

"I promise I'll do what I want to do."

"And that is?"

"I want to help..." he took a deep breath and his bottom lip trembled, "and I will," he said defiantly.

The deer had finally got his answer and was satisfied, so with a small nod of approval and a flick of his head he turned and galloped away, diving into the rhododendron bushes, which quivered violently as he disappeared. For a few seconds they were both silent, then Jason looked up at Ethan.

"This place is so cool," he said.

Ethan threw back his head and laughed; he'd never heard Heaven described in such a way before. Usually new arrivals were either too much in need of healing to notice their surroundings very much or they returned remembering it well and just smiled with delight at being home again safe and sound. Jason was a refreshing change and Ethan was beginning to enjoy his assignment. He smiled at Jason.

"It is different, isn't it?"

They carried on walking until they'd passed the small lake, then the path went uphill slightly and up some narrow stone steps. The sound of running water was much louder now and, as they reached the top step, the source of the noise became apparent. Running down between and over rocks and gullies was a sparkling brook, which bubbled and bounced in the sunlight, casting off rainbows as it went; the scent of the overhanging pine trees and the colours of the many plants that grew alongside the brook gave it a mysterious, almost magical, air - a place where you'd meet the little people and fairy folk. Jason's smile got even bigger when he saw it and he ran on ahead to dip his fingers into the crystal-clear water. Little boys and water on Earth could be a fatal combination but Ethan had no worries here, so he took his time to negotiate the narrower, twisting pathways in this part of the garden, keeping only one eye on his charge who was engrossed in following the water on its downhill journey. As he walked, Ethan felt Haniel's presence once more.

"The deer was a bit much," he said out loud, and she laughed.

"Oh, I don't know," she disagreed, cheerfully.

"Not very subtle."

"Sometimes the stick is of more use than the carrot," she replied, appearing by his side. He looked at her and found her eyes twinkling with mischief; he shook his head and decided he'd never figure out angels. "And I'll never be completely sure about humans either," she replied, reading his thoughts accurately again. She smiled and placed a hand on his arm, making him stop. "Look," she said, pointing up ahead.

Ethan followed her finger and frowned, seeing Jason motionless at the foot of the hill, his eyes fixed on the land on the other side of a small wood and metal red-coloured bridge. Ethan strained to see what had transfixed him, just making out a figure sitting under a weeping willow tree, but he couldn't see who it was. He glanced at Haniel who was smiling happily.

"Is that Tom?" he asked. She nodded without taking her eyes off Jason. Ethan turned back just as Jason looked up at him, an expression of happiness and disbelief on his small face.

"Yes, Jason, it's Tom," Ethan shouted, and his words gave Jason the courage - or permission - for which he was waiting. The boy turned towards the bridge and, with a cry of delight, began to run over it to his grandfather waiting on the other side.

Ethan didn't move to join them, not that he didn't want to, but this was a very private reunion on which he felt he shouldn't intrude. Haniel nodded.

"Yes, it's a joyous occasion and Jason has a lot to learn and remember. But then so have you." Ethan turned away from watching Tom pick up the excited seven-year old and looked at Haniel. He knew she was right - how boring it must be to be right all the time. "Not all the time, but this time I am." He smiled reluctantly and had to agree.

"Okay, this time. And I have learned a lot."

"Enough to guide someone full-time?" she asked. He shivered - that was the sixty-four million dollar question. Could he do this full-time?

"I'm not sure. Would I be helping a child?" he asked. She nodded.

"At first, yes. We have a lot of children like Jason who have taken on missions of great global importance at this time in Earth's life and they all need good guidance."

"And you think I'd be good enough for them?" he asked, not sure what her answer was going to be.

"I'm sure ... but you're not?"

"I didn't say that," he countered, frowning but pleased that she thought him worthy.

"No, but you didn't sound too confident either."

"I just wanted to know what I'm letting myself in for."

"Oh, is that all?" she replied haughtily. "Well then, you should have figured out by now that children are easier to guide than adults." He nodded, so she continued. "Many of the children born in these times are easier to guide because they have retained a lot of their knowledge of the spiritual worlds and what they have incarnated on Earth to do."

"Why is that?" Ethan asked.

"Because time on Earth is speeding up so they will not have the luxury of many years' spiritual practice to understand their life's purpose and soul path. They need to get a head start, one they will have earned by many previous lives dedicated to a more spiritual way of life. They are old souls who have important work to carry out to save the rest of their kind."

"Are humans in greater danger?" Ethan asked, surprised by the words. The archangel nodded.

"They are like a lot of other endangered species on the planet. But they endangered themselves as the problems are all man-made and Man has to solve them. No-one else can."

"Not even angels?"

She shook her head. "Not even angels. We are not allowed to interfere like that. If men kill the only home they have, then so be it. Their souls will return here and then go on to other worlds, planes and dimensions until all these lessons have been completed."

"And what happens to all the creatures of Earth?"

"Don't worry. The Earth itself will survive and the plants and creatures will recover, but mankind's fate is still firmly in his own hands and, in particular, the hands of the indigo and other special children."

Ethan considered her words carefully as he loved the Earth and didn't want to see mankind destroy itself; if he could do something to prevent that, then he was ready to give it a go.

"I want to help where I can," he said firmly, like Jason before him.

"Good," Haniel smiled. "Well then, after Jason is ready to go back to Earth, we can meet another child who is about to embark on its mission." Ethan had been hoping that he was to guide Jason but, from what she said, it didn't appear so. "No, not Jason," she replied, "but another soul just as worthy and beautiful."

"Who is it?" he asked, curious to know.

"Patience," Haniel said, "all in good time."

Ethan resigned himself to waiting, so he turned his gaze back to the boy and Tom who were now sitting together under the willow, and wondered what they were talking about.

CHAPTER 15

The Fox and the Wren

Jason sat leaning against his grandfather's chest in a hug he never wanted to relinquish. But he did have a question that he was burning to ask. He moved back far enough to see Tom's face when he asked it.

"Why did you leave me, Granddad?"

Tom didn't answer immediately but continued to gaze into the distance, a small smile on his serene face. "I haven't left you, Jason," he said at last.

"But you're here," Jason said indignantly, angry that Tom wasn't being straight with him. Tom took his hand.

"Yes, I am, Jason," he said quietly, "but then so are you." Jason frowned, not understanding what he was saying, and Tom smiled down at him. "Let me try to explain," he continued, pausing to think how to say this in a way a seven-year old would get it, as the concepts weren't easy. "Now, you know I love you, don't you?" Jason nodded. "Then I'll always love you whether I'm on Earth or not. Love can never be lost, and when people return here they still care about those left on Earth. I still love you and watch over you all the time."

Jason's eyes got bigger. "You do?"

"Oh, I do," Tom laughed. "I saw you rescue that frog from Mrs Smith's cat the other day and I was so proud of you." Jason gasped, as he hadn't told anyone about that yet Granddad Tom knew.

"You saw me?" he asked. Tom nodded.

"Yes, I'm with you a lot and I wish you'd get on with your life. I haven't left you, I'm just in another place."

"But I miss you," Jason replied, trying hard to stop his bottom lip from quivering.

"I know you do, but we can still talk to each other just like we are doing now."

"How?" Jason demanded.

"It's simple," Tom said. "All you have to do is go somewhere quiet, sit down and call me in your head, then think of this spot - this can be our meeting place."

"I just think of this tree and you'll be here?" the boy frowned, as that didn't sound too hard to do at all.

"That's right. You can do that, can't you?"

"I can do that," Jason confirmed confidently with a smile.

"Then we'll never have to be apart again, will we?"

"That's cool, Granddad," he whispered, relaxing back into his chest once more.

Tom sighed inwardly, wishing the rest of Jason's life would be as simple as this. He had seen more than one future for his grandson and some of them were far from pleasant, but as always there was one possible, perfect future. It was the highest one can attain in any given lifetime, possible to achieve but not an easy task at all. There are many obstacles on a person's pathway and with each obstacle there are choices to be made to overcome them; these choices could set one on a completely different direction to one's chosen soul path, or cause delays or send one up a dead end. Without guidance, it can become an impenetrable maze that cannot be escaped from. Life on Earth is fraught with difficulties, more now than ever before, solely because there are so many choices, maybe too many. Never before in human history can people choose so much, such as where they live, their career, further training, their lifestyle, their partner and even their own personal style. Is it any wonder that some get lost and confused on the way?

If Jason would let him, Tom hoped to help him make his choices wisely, to his highest good and the highest good of all those around him, for he had an important role to play in Earth's history. But with every problem he faced, there was a chance he'd stray off track. He had also chosen to 'work off' some karma with the new soul that was Gerry Rice; it wouldn't be easy, as this soul wasn't going to understand him at all. Jason had his work cut out to remain on friendly terms with his father yet stay on his chosen route, but then he had known that before he agreed to incarnate again.

'Maybe I can make all the difference,' Tom thought, but he also knew the limits within which he had to stay. He might have been given permission to be a guide for Jason but that didn't mean he could make his choices for him and there were rules by which to abide even in Heaven. Tom stroked Jason's hair and wished they could have longer together, but there was someone else Jason had to meet before returning to Earth and, even though he was loath to disturb their quiet conversation, he had to. He patted Jason on the shoulder.

"I'd like you to come with me to meet someone very special."

Jason looked up at him, all wide-eyed and innocent. "Okay, Granddad, who is it?"

"I don't want to spoil the surprise," he smiled, then added, "You, young man, will just have to be patient."

"As long as I'm with you, Granddad."

Tom felt a wave of emotion at the love and trust Jason had in him and felt humbled by it. "You are such a fine boy, Jason," he said. "You make me very proud." Jason didn't know what to say in reply, so he just smiled as they climbed to their feet. They started back over the ornamental bridge and, hand in hand, went up the path into the wider reaches of the gardens. Ethan saw them leave and wasn't sure what he should do.

"You must go too," Haniel told him, "so that you can return Jason - he doesn't have too much longer before he must go back." Ethan nodded his understanding and began to follow them out of the Chinese garden and into woods full of tall, majestic trees.

'Where are they going?' he wondered, but he got no answers. He carried on, keeping the pair of them in sight.

The light coming through the leafy canopy made patterns on the forest floor. It was a cool haven after the earlier warmth and Jason liked the woods as they reminded him of the many times he and Tom had walked the protected ancient woodland near their home. He especially loved bluebell time when there was a carpet of lavender-blue dancing happily under the huge trunks of the oaks and beeches; it was magical and this wood was just like that. Although it wasn't the season for bluebells on Earth, they were in their full glory here and Jason sighed with pleasure; Tom smiled, it was so nice to have this chance to walk together one last time in their favourite environment. Tom looked down at his beloved grandson then up ahead, where he knew that Jason's totem animal was waiting for them. A flash of red caught his eye and he followed the movement until he saw him, wondering how Jason would react when he introduced them. He steered him down a smaller side path to the clearing where the meeting would take place; as they weaved between some tree trunks with Jason now in the lead, Tom watched him carefully as he burst into the clearing and came abruptly to a halt. Sitting calmly there was a large, red fox with a white breast and a magnificent bushy tail. Jason stared at him, expecting him to run away, but this fox had no intention of doing that. Instead, it spoke.

"Hello."

Jason let out a small gasp and turned to find reassurance from Tom.

"It's okay, Jason, he won't hurt you." Jason glanced back at the fox, who sat quite still, his amber eyes holding a spark of amusement. "Go and talk to him," Tom encouraged. Jason nodded and moved very cautiously a little closer to the animal, who didn't appear to mind him at all. Jason coughed politely.

"Hello, I'm Jason."

The fox appeared to nod. "I know."

"You do?" Jason exclaimed.

"Yes, I do, and I've been waiting for you."

"Why?" the boy frowned, unsure what the fox was talking about.

"I'm your totem animal," the fox replied importantly and Jason's frown deepened.

"Totem…?"

"That's right."

"What's a totem?" Jason asked, never having heard that word before. He thought he heard the fox sigh before he began his explanation.

"A totem is a symbol of the connection between the spirit world here and a life being lived on Earth." Jason was none the wiser and Tom smiled as it was not easy to understand, since totems are energy beings and not physical. The fox knew he hadn't made it clear enough for Jason, so he tried again. "I am a fox and my energies are cunning, adaptability, observation, swiftness of thought, action and invisibility." Jason's ears pricked up at that last quality.

"Invisibility?" he asked. "You can be invisible?"

The fox scratched his ear with a paw before he replied. "I can't exactly become invisible but I can merge into my surroundings so no-one sees me. You can learn from me to do this too." Jason thought he'd like to do that and could think of more than one occasion he would have loved to vanish into the wallpaper.

"Really, you can teach me?" he asked, his blue eyes as big as saucers.

The fox nodded. "I can, but it takes practice. Are you prepared for that?"

"Yes, if I can vanish when I need to, I'll practise loads and loads," he agreed earnestly, thinking how nice it would be to escape his father's penetrating eyes.

"Then I shall help you and I will be nearby when you ask for help. Learn about me and my abilities and there'll be many times when I can give my energies to your cause. Be adaptable, as I am, and you will be able to turn disasters into triumphs, adversity into opportunity. You have many gifts, my friend, and I will help you."

Tom nudged Jason, who stood there with his mouth open, taking his time to memorise what the fox had told him. "Jason, we have to go now. Thank the fox and then we have to leave."

The boy looked up at his grandfather. "So soon, Granddad?"

"I'm afraid so."

Jason sighed heavily then turned back to the patient fox. "Thank you for being my toting animal." The fox raised one eyebrow and corrected him.

"Totem animal," he said haughtily.

"Sorry," Jason apologised.

"Quite alright," the fox replied. Tom smothered the urge to laugh. Instead he nodded his thanks to the fox and guided his grandson out of the clearing, back to the main path where Ethan was waiting.

"Have you had a good time, Jason?" he asked, noting that there was a sparkle about him that hadn't been there earlier. Jason nodded, a big smile on his impish face.

"This is Granddad Tom," he said and the older man smiled at his grown-up introduction.

"I sort of guessed he was," Ethan said lightly. He didn't want to rain on Jason's parade but his time was now up and he had to go, even though he wouldn't want to. They walked together back out of the forest and into the Japanese garden with Jason happily skipping in front of them.

"He looks so happy," Ethan said quietly.

"Um, he does, but he has to leave now, doesn't he?"

Ethan nodded. "Shall I tell him or will you?"

"I guess I will," Tom sighed. Ethan was glad about that, as he knew how upset Jason might be at parting from his beloved grandfather again and it wasn't very easy to tell a child what they don't want to hear.

"I'll go on across the bridge then," Ethan said. As he caught up with the boy, he told him that his grandfather needed to speak to him. Jason's face was puckered up into a frown when he returned to Tom's side by the willow tree where they had first met.

"What's wrong, Granddad?" he asked.

"Nothing's wrong, Jason, except that you have to go home with Ethan now."

"But I don't want to. Can't I stay here with you?"

Tom gathered Jason into his arms. "I wish you could but it's not your time yet," he said huskily, trying to prevent his emotions getting the better of him. "You remember what you promised to the deer?"

Jason pulled back in surprise. "You know about that?"

"Of course I know. I told you I keep a good eye on you, so you'd better behave yourself or there'll be trouble." Jason grinned and somehow felt better, knowing Tom was watching over him. "So, are you going to be good and return to Earth to carry out your promise?"

"I suppose so," the boy said reluctantly. "But you will help me, won't you?"

"A promise is a promise," Tom nodded. "I said I'd be here whenever you need to speak to me and I will, right here, remember?"

"Yes, I remember."

"So, you know how to get in touch with me?"

Jason nodded then he thought of something else. "But, Granddad, how will I know when you want to talk to me?" Tom hadn't thought of that, but it would indeed be very helpful if he did have a way of attracting Jason's attention, especially if he were in some kind of danger.

"I'm not sure. What do you reckon would make you think I was calling you?" Jason didn't have to think too hard to come up with an answer.

"A Jenny Wren," he said, smiling as he remembered how excited Tom always got whenever he saw one. Although they are tiny, they are also bold and sing beautifully, as they flit in and out of the foliage, their chocolate-brown feathers like velvet. Tom held out his hand

and, in a second, there was a fluttering of tiny wings and a wren appeared on his hand. Jason gasped in delight and Tom laughed.

"She is so beautiful," Jason whispered, afraid he might scare her away.

"You don't have to whisper. The animals here are not in any danger like they are on Earth, so like the deer and the fox she has no fear of us. Do you?" he said to the petite bird, happily perched on his index finger. It looked at them both with its button eye and flicked up its tail at a characteristic jaunty angle.

"No fear, no fear."

"Wow," Jason said in awe. He had never been so close to a wren before; usually, he was lucky to get a fleeting glimpse of one as it disappeared into a hedgerow.

"Would you like her to sit on your hand?" Tom asked him.

Jason's expression was a picture of astonishment and longing. "Really?" he exclaimed, "she'd do that?" Tom looked at the wren who nodded once, bobbed up and down on her spindly legs and jumped onto Jason's shaking hand as he held it out. "Oh boy, she's so cool," he said quietly. He took a few minutes to study her in detail; she was perfect, even more beautiful up close than he'd ever imagined. He sighed with pleasure and finally managed to tear his eyes away from her and back to his grandfather. "So will she come to me when you need to talk to me?"

"Why don't you ask her yourself?" Tom replied.

Jason held his hand up so he was eye to eye with the wren. "Will you come to me when Granddad needs me?" he asked in a very serious, grown-up voice. The wren bobbed up and down again before she spoke.

"I send one to you."

"She is the archetype of all the wrens on Earth, their spirit," Tom explained. "Do you understand?"

Jason thought he did. "Like the deer," he said.

"Exactly, they are representatives of all the wrens and deer on Earth. So now when you see a wren and it comes to you, you'll know why."

Jason nodded. "Then I'll sit down and think of this tree and…"

"…we'll all be together again," Tom finished for him.

"So be it," the wren said clearly, and with a final bob and a flick of her tail she flew away.

As much as he wanted to, Tom couldn't put off his parting from his grandson any longer, so he crouched down and looked him in the eye.

"It's time, Jason," he said, and even though his bottom lip quivered, Jason nodded and they embraced. Tom held him tightly, knowing this would be the last time for many years that he'd be able to do this. When Jason visited him again, the connection wouldn't be this clear or strong; Tom knew this and hoped that Jason would still be able to communicate with him. It wasn't going to be quite as easy as it may have sounded, but his guides would help and somehow he was sure they'd get through. Jason had a hill to climb in this lifetime but he had chosen it and, with a little advice and encouragement, he could do all he had set out to do. When he let him go, a single tear ran down Jason's face but he didn't brush it away.

"I'll come and see you again soon, Granddad."

"You do that," Tom said, trying to keep his voice from cracking. Jason turned and began to walk to the bridge where Ethan waited. As he got there, he turned and waved to Tom before carrying on. Tom smiled and raised his hand in a final goodbye, then they moved on until he couldn't see them anymore.

★

CHAPTER 16

School Over

Ethan looked at the solemn little boy, who remained quiet as they made their way out of the Japanese garden and into the English one. He hadn't spoken since leaving Tom and, as they got nearer and nearer to the exit gate, Ethan began to worry. Perhaps this hadn't been a good idea after all; maybe Jason felt worse now than if he'd never come on this trip to Heaven, as it must be like losing Tom all over again. Finally, he couldn't bear the silence any longer.

"Jason, are you okay? I mean, I know it's upsetting to have to leave your granddad again but…" Jason looked up at him and, to his great relief, he was smiling.

"It's fine, Ethan. I know now he hasn't left me and I can talk to him when I need to."

Ethan returned his smile, happy that he hadn't made things worse. "That's right. You never lose anyone you love – they're just somewhere different."

"I was just thinking about all the things I've seen," the boy continued. Ethan wondered how, at only seven, he was going to deal with it all but, again, Jason surprised him. "You know," he said, "I really do know what I want to do with my life now and no-one is going to stop me."

"Oh dear," Ethan grinned, thinking of someone who wasn't going to be too pleased about that. Jason didn't need him to explain. He knew exactly the problems he and his father were going to have, but he also knew what he had to do for his soul's growth and his own happiness. It wasn't going to be a comfortable ride but he was prepared to take it. No more needed to be said. They went out of the gate and in no time at all were back at the vortex.

"When we get back, it'll be like you've just left," Ethan said and Jason smiled.

"Good, I'm hungry."

Ethan licked his lips, remembering the picnic that was being laid out and regretting that he couldn't partake of some of it. "You're lucky," he said grudgingly and Jason grinned, pleased to have one advantage over his tour guide. Ethan took his hand and, with a nod, they both stepped into the vortex.

"Wheee…" Jason shouted, as they slid down as if on a slide at a funfair. It was great fun but all too soon it was over and they found themselves standing next to Jason's body, which still sat looking into space. Ethan watched Jason's reaction to seeing himself, expecting him to be perturbed by it, but they boy wasn't bothered at all. If anything, he looked rather disparagingly at it, with little concern.

"Well, Jason, I have to leave you now."

"Thank you, Ethan, for taking me to see Granddad."

"I hope you learned some valuable lessons about death. It isn't the end of life, just another way, a different place. But Tom still loves you."

"And I can still speak with him."

"Any time," Ethan smiled. "Now, do you remember how you got out of your body?"

Jason wasn't sure. "I closed my eyes and counted to ten?" he asked and Ethan nodded.

"That's right, so that's how you get back in, okay?"

"Right. Will I ever see you again?"

"Maybe." Ethan wasn't sure. "But you don't need me. You've already got your own guide and the fox and Granddad Tom."

"I have a guide like you?" Jason was surprised.

"Everyone does and, before you ask, all you have to do is ask her to show herself to you when you sit quietly and she will. Then you can get to know each other just like we have."

"Cool." Jason was impressed by the notion.

"Yep, it's cool. You have lots of help if you ask for it. But now, young man, you have a picnic to eat and I have more work to do."

"Okay", Jason said reluctantly and closed his eyes. "One, two, three…" he began and slowly his etheric form slipped into his physical body. Ethan made sure he had returned fully before he too became invisible. Jason jerked once and looked around, but Ethan was nowhere to be seen. Yet, for the first time since Granddad Tom died, he felt hope - and he was hungry.

"Jason, come and have something to eat." His mother's voice sounded strained as she'd been very worried about him; he had lost weight but recently food just hadn't interested him at all. Now he got up and made his way to the picnic. "Sit here, dear." His mother made room for him on the chequered rug and handed him a plate of delicacies. His stomach rumbled and his mouth watered at the sight of some of his personal favourites that she had obviously made just to try and tempt him into eating. He didn't need any tempting at all now.

"Thanks, Mum," he said and bit into a chocolate éclair, sending cream squirting out of the end all over his baby sister. For a moment he froze, thinking he'd get told off, but his mother's face twitched once then she laughed. And suddenly they were all laughing just like they used to. Ethan watched the scene and smiled.

"He'll be alright," Haniel said in his ear.

"I know," he replied, taking one last long look at the food he couldn't have, before he turned away and ascended back to the circular building overlooking Earth.

They sat once more upon the marble benches and for a few moments neither spoke. It was Haniel who broke the silence.

"Well, Ethan, you are now ready to guide a soul on their Earth walk," she said. Ethan turned in surprise.

"You think so?"

"Yes," she laughed, "we think you are. After all, you've done very well helping Kathleen, Ben and Jason - or don't you agree?"

"I think I did," he said hesitantly.

"You did," she confirmed and Ethan relaxed. "So, what's the problem? Are you or are you not ready now, this instant, to be a guide?" He still wasn't one hundred per cent sure he was but he was willing to give it his all if someone were prepared to let him, so he nodded.

"Yes, Haniel, I think I'm ready."

"Hallelujah," she said loudly, "finally, you have some faith in yourself."

"I guess I do," he smiled.

"It's about time," she said, shaking her head. "We have so much more belief in your abilities than you do. I can assure you it's very frustrating seeing you hold back, scared to put a foot wrong so you don't have a chance to succeed."

"But if I do something wrong as a guide, I could really screw up big-time."

"In theory you could but because you know that, you won't."

"Why won't I?"

"Because you'll think carefully before you act and you'll look at problems from all angles, see all possible outcomes before using your powers as a guide."

"Aha," he said, as the penny finally dropped. "I see what you mean." "Wonderful," she laughed. "Ethan, we have many who train to be guides and who think they'll be great at it. They know it all and are supremely confident in their own abilities. Do you think they would make good guides?" She looked at him with one eyebrow raised and he shook his head.

"Probably not," he said.

"You're probably right," she replied. "Just have enough confidence to support your charge. But never, never take their challenges away from them and always open up their vision. Remember, this universe is boundless and there are always more possibilities. Help them to see that and then let them make their own choices and decisions. That's all there is to it." He gulped and she smiled. "So, how about we find you a soul to guide?"

He was stunned. "What, now?"

"Yes now, or is there some reason not to?" she countered.

"But I haven't finished school yet."

She laughed. "Do you think you'll learn any more there than you've just learned?" she asked him. He didn't have to think too hard about that to realise she was right - yet again - and he had learned so much that at least he now knew what not to do. "And the rest comes with practice," she said. He nodded.

"You're right, there's no time like the present. I'm ready," he said with conviction.

"Thank God," she replied and, in a flash, they disappeared from the Observatory and reappeared in the Hall of Records, standing on the mezzanine that went around the study area of the great Hall.

Below them were three people who were preparing lesson plans for their next incarnation and helping them were the Lights of Purpose, beings who guided souls in the right direction for their greatest spiritual development in a single lifetime. You could never learn it all in one trip on the merry-go-round, but there was always the opportunity for a maximum advancement in each lifetime. Sadly, few managed to reach that but there was always more than one chance to achieve enlightenment. Haniel surveyed the scene and turned to Ethan.

"So here we have three souls, all in need of a guide. They have already been assigned gatekeepers but a gatekeeper's job is a little different to a guide's, isn't it?"

Ethan nodded. Some called their gatekeepers 'guardian angels' or protectors, which is what they are, but they also allow the soul to enter the spirit world to receive guidance while keeping out dark spirits that might try to enter the physical world through their

149

charge. Possession could happen if the gatekeeper were not vigilant or if the soul strayed onto a path of darkness.

Ethan looked down, trying to see where the protectors were, as they should stay close by their charges from the moment they were chosen until the soul under their protection returned safely to Heaven. He spotted them standing and observing by one of the many bookcases that filled the rest of the space. One was a tall, slim man of Nordic appearance, another a Japanese soldier and the third an elegant lady dressed in a deep-blue crinoline dress. She looked so fragile and delicate, not what most people might expect their protector to look like, but she didn't need a sword or armour to be a formidable opponent to any entity that threatened her charge. She must have felt their presence, as she looked up at them and smiled; she was a beauty and Ethan smiled back. Haniel chuckled to herself. She understood the power of a beautiful face and its effect on others but it was an illusion, so she coughed once and Ethan returned his attention to the job in hand.

"Right then, these souls have nearly finished their life plans. One is going to attempt to learn patience and humility. This soul is quite young." The way she said that gave Ethan the impression that although the soul was as perfect as the others, he still had a long way to go.

"Not him then," he muttered under his breath.

"The other two," Haniel continued, "will be rather special children. Both are old, experienced souls whose time on Earth is to be used to improve the situation there. They have both almost completed their own life lessons although they each have one karmic debt to repay. But on the whole they are free of most baggage and are willing and able to work on higher goals."

"And you want me to help one of them?" he asked, having a fair idea of her answer.

"Yes, if you wish to."

"Okay then," he replied, knowing that she would be pleased. "So, which one?"

"That is your decision. But ultimately you will know once you read what each one has decided to do on their life ahead."

"Then I get to read their life plans?"

"Yes, it is essential you know their intended destinations as they will remember only fragments once they incarnate. It is part of your job to encourage them on the paths that will help them fulfil their goals - and steer them away from courses of action that won't."

"Do I meet them now or what?"

She shook her head. "No, you'll wait 'til they incarnate then read their life plans. The one you should choose will become apparent." He looked dubious and she laughed. "It will, I promise." He couldn't say that she didn't keep her promises, so he nodded.

"Right then, I wait and then what?"

"You watch and listen. The best time to make your acquaintance with your charge is in early childhood. Many so-called imaginary friends are in fact guides getting to know their charges."

"How should I appear so that I don't frighten them?"

She smiled. "I think you'll find your answer to that in the life plan. It will also contain a short biography of previous lives and you may be surprised what you discover." He hated it when she went all cryptic on him but he knew he'd find out soon enough what she meant; she wasn't going to tell him, that was for sure. He had to work hard for his answers.

As time moves differently in Heaven, in no time at all the three souls had left to begin their journeys along with their protectors, and it was only then that Ethan and Haniel walked down the spiral staircase to the main floor of the Hall of Records and to the table where the Akashic books were open waiting for them.

Ethan picked up the nearest book and began to read. This soul had lived hundreds of lives stretching back to Atlantis, in many historic times and places and in a variety of guises. He had been alive at the time of Christ in Palestine and had even seen him preach. He'd been a slave in Rome, a noble woman in the Middle Ages, an artist in Paris and many more in between. In the last life, she had been a pioneer in alternative medicine and instrumental in reintroducing reflexology to the western world. This time around, the soul was to incarnate as a male and had set himself the task of using new technology for the betterment of the environment; he was to promote new ways of generating power that didn't produce waste or damage the world with polluting bi-products. He would see new ways of doing things and be inspiring enough to make a difference where it really counted, at governmental and corporate levels. Ethan found this admirable and wished him luck, but didn't feel that he could help too much in achieving this goal.

He shook his head and looked up at Haniel who was smiling back at him. Ethan had that feeling again. She'd said he had a choice and, in a way, he did; yet in another he didn't, as she already knew which one he'd choose before he'd even read the first words in the records. He resisted the temptation to complain and picked up the other book.

'I hate being played,' he thought, and she laughed.

With a smile on his handsome face, he began to read. First he studied the past and had a surprise, as Haniel had said he would. A few hundred years ago Ethan had lived as a Native American called Running Elk in the northern plains of what are now the Dakotas. He had enjoyed a life of great spirituality, as both a seer and a provider for his people, and in that life he had been fortunate to marry a young squaw from a neighbouring tribe called Heyola. Together, their love produced four strong, healthy children and they had had a long and happy life. It had been a time of living in harmony with Mother Earth, of communicating with the plants and animals to learn their wisdom and use them with respect and love. He looked up at Haniel with tears in his eyes.

"Is it really her?" he whispered.

She nodded. "Yes, Ethan, it is." It had been one of his happiest lifetimes and she had been his greatest love; now he had the chance to guide her on another great journey. He had always longed to meet this soul again but until now his wish hadn't been granted.

"Why was that?" he asked Haniel.

"Because you both had other things to do, other people to meet and learn from. What you had then could never be repeated, although the bond you have with this soul will be important if you choose to guide her."

He smiled sadly. "You already know I will," he said.

"Then you should read on and find out what your charge will be up against."

He didn't like the sound of that and picked up the book to read on. She was to incarnate into a family that wasn't particularly different to hundreds of others, middle class and average; but she would be anything but, as she was a special child on a mission. Ethan's eyebrows rose sharply as he read what that was: born with a range of powers, including clairvoyance and healing, she would strive to show others that they could live in peace together and in harmony with the planet. Her long-term aim was to set up her own spiritual eco-community, to be an example of living lightly on the Earth; and although it could be done more easily now, with the advances of technology, than ever before in human history, to get there wasn't going to be all plain sailing. Her family were not at all in tune with her or her powers, which would be a big challenge, and she also had some karma to work off with her mother. But her goals were possible and the rewards for her soul growth would be huge. Ethan smiled.

'And with me on her side,' he thought, 'how can she go wrong?'

Haniel laughed and clapped him on the hack. "Yes, right, but remember that there are rules that must not be broken."

"I know and I'll be very careful."

"Good, and remember too that there is always help available for you - just ask." He nodded and, at last, felt confident that he could do a good job. Haniel sighed with relief. "It's about time," she said, "because I think you just graduated."

He suddenly understood just how far he had come and that he had passed another test on his own journey to enlightenment. Now another challenge awaited him and he was ready, willing and eager to begin. She smiled happily, as her work with Ethan was all but done.

"Do you know, Ethan," she asked, "why angels have wings?"

He shook his head. "No, I don't."

"Because we take ourselves lightly."

For a few seconds he had to think about that, then he laughed. "I'll try to as well," he told her.

"Good, because you'll need a sense of humour to be a great guide." She saw him start at that and she laughed. "You'll find out soon enough," was all she'd say before she vanished.

Ethan had a feeling she'd be right again and settled down to watch over his new charge until they were ready to meet.

If you have enjoyed this book...

Local Legend is committed to publishing the very best spiritual writing, both fiction and non-fiction. You might also enjoy:

SIMPLY SPIRITUAL

Jacqui Rogers (ISBN 978-1-907203-75-6)

The 'spookies' started contacting Jacqui when she was a child and never gave up until, at last, she developed her psychic talents and became the successful international medium she is now. This is a powerful and moving account of her difficult life and her triumph over adversity, with many great stories of her spiritual readings.

The book was a Finalist in The People's Book Prize national awards.

AURA CHILD

A I Kaymen (ISBN 978-1-907203-71-8)

One of the most astonishing books ever written, telling the true story of a genuine indigo child. Genevieve grew up in a normal London family but from an early age realised that she had very special spiritual and psychic gifts. She saw the energy fields around living things, read people's thoughts and even found herself slipping through time, able to converse with the spirits of those who had lived in her neighbourhood. This is an uplifting and inspiring book for what it tells us about the nature of our minds.

THE QUIRKY MEDIUM

Alison Wynne-Ryder (ISBN 978-1-907203-47-3)

Alison is the co-host of the TV show *Rescue Mediums*, in which she puts herself in real danger to free homes of lost and often malicious spirits. Yet she is a most reluctant medium, afraid of ghosts! This is her amazing and often very funny autobiography, taking us 'back stage' of the television production as well as describing how she came to discover the psychic gifts that have brought her an international following.

Winner of the Silver Medal in the national Wishing Shelf Book Awards.

CELESTIAL AMBULANCE

Ann Matkins (ISBN 978-1-907203-45-9)

A brave and delightful comedy novel. Having died of cancer, Ben wakes up in the afterlife looking forward to a good rest, only to find that everyone is expected to get a job! He becomes the driver of an ambulance (with a mind of her own), rescuing the spirits of others who have died suddenly and delivering them safely home. This book is as thought-provoking as it is entertaining.

TAP ONCE FOR YES

Jacquie Parton (ISBN 978-1-907203-62-6)

This extraordinary book offers powerful evidence of human survival after death. When Jacquie's son Andrew suddenly committed suicide, she was devastated. But she was determined to find out whether his spirit lived on, and began to receive incredible yet undeniable messages from him... Several others also then described deliberate attempts at spirit contact. This is a story of astonishing love and courage, as Jacquie fought her own grief and others' doubts in order to prove to the world that her son still lives.

5P1R1T R3V3L4T10N5

Nigel Peace (ISBN 978-1-907203-14-5)

With descriptions of more than a hundred proven prophetic dreams and many more everyday synchronicities, the author shows us that, without doubt, we can know the future and that everyone can receive genuine spiritual guidance for our lives' challenges. World-renowned biologist Dr Rupert Sheldrake has endorsed this book as "...vivid and fascinating... pioneering research..." and it was national runner-up in The People's Book Prize awards.

RAINBOW CHILD

S L Coyne (ISBN 978-1-907203-92-3)

Beautifully written in language that is alternately lyrical and childlike, this is the story of young Rebekah and the people she discovers as her family settles in a new town far from their familiar home. As dark family secrets begin to unravel, her life takes many turns both delightful and terrifying as the story builds to a tragic and breathless climax that just keeps on going. This book shows us how we look at others who are 'different'. Through the eyes of Rebekah, writing equally with passion and humour, we see the truth of human nature...

These titles are all available as paperbacks and eBooks.
Further details and extracts of these and many
other beautiful books may be seen at
www.local-legend.co.uk

Lightning Source UK Ltd.
Milton Keynes UK
UKOW04f0125071114

241199UK00007B/161/P